DON'T SMELL THE FLOSS

STORIES BY MATTY BYLOOS

A Write Bloody Book
Nashville. Los Angeles. USA

WRITE BLOODY PUBLISHING
NASHVILLE, TN

Don't Smell the Floss
by Matty Byloos

Write Bloody Publishing ©2009.
1ˢᵗ printing.
Printed in NASHVILLE, TN USA

Don't Smell the Floss Copyright 2009. All Rights Reserved.

Published by Write Bloody Publishing.

Printed in Tennessee, USA.

Cover Designed by Paul Smith   smithers.carbonmade.com
Interior Layout by Lea C. Deschenes   quantumredhead.com
Type set in Helvetica Neue and Bell MT
Edited by Derrick Brown, shea M gauer, Saadia Byram,
Michael Sarnowski and Keion Moradi
Proofread by Jennifer Roach

To contact the author, send an email to writebloody@gmail.com

THANKS

In no special order, I wish to thank Derrick Brown;
all the Editors of this book; Benjamin Weissman; Beyond
Baroque, my old Monday Night Fiction Writing Crew and
Fred Dewey; the Smalldoggies Family; Jon Furmanski;
Michael Marcus; Casey McKinney and the Fanzine;
Andrew Leland and the Believer; William Mitchell; my
new Tuesday Fiction Writing Group that's been super
wonderful (Keion, Adam, Vilma, Claudia, Rhea, Drew,
Ixchel, Ben, Chris, Justin, Liz, Chris and Cathy); my
sister and parents; the Hammer Museum New American
Writing Series; the Write Bloody Crew of Writers; Sam
Stern; Julian Hoeber; Maggie Wells; Lesley Worton;
Nate Collins; Kyle Holm; Adrew Ullrich; Leah Rico; all
of my neighbors for letting me spy on them for the sake of
good fiction material; Stephen Tourell; Tom Burkett; Alex
Wagman; April Durham; Darcelle Bleau; Jenny Baxton;
Victoria Morrow; Dennis Cooper; John Mandel; Neil
Mooney; and anyone else who ever shared something with
me that was skewed completely out of proportion and then
recast as the words or experience of one of these ridiculous
fictional characters....

This book is dedicated to my sister, who is my BFFF.

DON'T SMELL THE FLOSS

PART ONE

KITTIED TO DEATH: LOVE STORIES FOR A CONTEMPORARY AUDIENCE

ONE DAY, LETTER FROM GHOST LEG

I have a videotape. I watch this videotape over and over again, every night, by myself. I make coffee, which never comes out right. Achievement, as a concept, weighs on me incessantly. The coffee, too dark or not dark enough, thinned and hazy with nonfat milk, or turned pale-white with heavy cream; it's never perfect. I have tried to find consistency in this drink, tried too hard at what has become the impossible, and I have failed miserably. Perseverance in the face of adversity can yield achievement. Beauty for its own sake, entirely. A perfect cup of coffee could signify a degree of over-achievement. I drink my bad coffee and watch my video tape.

I have had this dream since I was eleven; every night, mostly, the same dream. It's about becoming whole. I feel there's an alien aspect to my body. I take steps to improve this in the dream, steps that any normal person would understand to be extreme. There is a persistent itch in the index finger of my right hand. I stare at the finger twitching uncontrollably, almost imperceptibly, for hours in my dream. I watch the finger for weeks at a time: I have lost countless jobs in this dream, in these dreams, because I spend all my time watching the finger. Then I hack it off. It is a wonderment how much effort it requires to do the banal: to scratch the itch, you might say—but there it is—the effort, and the release. It is done, the finger gone. With this solution in place, a mild collapse ensues. Eventually, even the most bland installment of a handshake with a stranger becomes my victory.

Medical researchers have identified three groups within the larger community of people obsessed with amputation:

1.) *"Pretenders" use wheelchairs, crutches and other devices to make people think they are disabled.*

2.) *"Devotees" are sexually attracted to people with amputations and disabled people, and will often search for them on the Internet.*

3.) *"Wannabees," who get the most attention, live for the removal of their healthy limbs.*

My world exists beneath a wet blanket of sorts, damp-muted, slightly hazy and mostly gone gray. It is morning. I pace the apartment, recounting the same dream from the night before, dragging my feet across the carpet, which is trying hard to still look chocolate brown. After years of weekly spills cleaned up with bleach, the rug looks more yellow or olive drab than chocolate, slowly entering the realm of brown camouflage. Between my toes a dampness—the echo of a spill that has not entirely dried. I fake-hobble around, clutching my right leg behind me like a pirate. The feeling of my curled foot in my hand. There is a stain in the rug in front of the bathroom that looks like a dead jellyfish, a blobby mass sunken into the carpet with entrails curling off in another direction. Today is not unlike any other day; there is always the opportunity for achievement, there is always pleasure to be found in the idea of asymmetry. Beauty for beauty's sake: perhaps it is what the world needs. In the bathroom, I brush my teeth, rinse, spit, and towel off my tingling mouth. I stand in the mirror with my teeth clenched until I can hardly recognize myself anymore, cheeks hardened and white in the middle, small apples turned inside-out, eyes bulging, froggish. Several seconds go by. Maybe minutes. I ask the toothbrush why this has just happened. What could it mean to be a person alone, holding my breath in the mirror? I hear the toothbrush mumbling something incoherent. I never bother to clarify.

Statistics and Hearsay Concerning Amputation

Healthy people seeking amputations are nowhere near as rare as one might think. In May of 1998, a seventy-nine-year-old man from New York traveled to Mexico and paid $10,000 for a black-market leg amputation; he died of gangrene in a motel. In October of 1999, a mentally competent man in Milwaukee severed his arm with a homemade guillotine, and then threatened to sever it again if surgeons reattached it. That same month a legal investigator for the California State Bar, after being refused a hospital amputation, tied off her legs with tourniquets

*and began to pack them in ice, hoping that gangrene would set
in, necessitating an amputation. She passed out and ultimately
gave up. Now she says she will probably have to lie under a train,
or shoot her legs off with a shotgun.*

Every morning, I drink my bad coffee, think about
my dream from the night before, and replay in my head
the dubious aspects of my childhood, which I believe to be
directly responsible for my present condition, interjecting
within this steady stream of mental images some of my
fonder memories from my video. I sit, tentatively, on my
couch in the living room. This morning is quiet, feels older,
moves slower and less awkwardly. It is not gawky and
reckless like other mornings; instead, it is more pubescent
teenager in appearance. I notice the window to my left is
open. The broken blinds near the top of the window frame
always look like a bundle of tied-up sticks. To protect
the room from the glare of the sun would be a miracle in
their present condition. A miracle represents the opposite
of achievement, and thus I deem it uninteresting. With
a miracle, there is reward without effort, an impossible
answer given with no time spent struggling with the
question. The morning air is chilled, tinged with foggy
haze, and moves past the window too fast. Occasionally,
bits of fog appear in the room with me, blown in through
the opening near the bottom of the window. They take
shape, remain uncompromised in their clusters of frosted
white, making it difficult to see from one side of the room
to the other at times. Add to this, the steam from my coffee,

far too creamy this morning, with more the pre-fab smell of Twinkies than the actual taste of coffee.

I have thought through the circumstances of my childhood relentlessly. Perhaps I have been too hard on myself. I place numerous restrictions on my diet. I cleanse my liver with milk thistle and oil of clove; detoxify my spleen and kidneys with mixtures of honey, cayenne pepper, and apple vinegar; grind lime skins with raw garlic for my intestines. I conduct copious amounts of research on anesthesia and wound control. I take steps to educate myself in the field of occupational prosthetics at the local college. I go to great lengths to transfer my condition to a more socially viable and acceptable form, offering countless hours of volunteer work with the handicapped. I have had several uncomfortable conversations with psychologists and surgeons known to be specialists in the care of pre-surgical and post-operative transsexuals. Mine is not an aesthetic need; this visceral compunction towards functional asymmetry is *who I am….*

A Clinical Definition of Apotemnophilia:

From the Greek, literally meaning "amputation love." Succinctly, apotemnophilia defines the condition of self-demand amputation, which is believed to be related to the eroticization of the stump and to overachievement despite a handicap. The apotemnophiliac obsession represents an *idée fixe* rather than a paranoid delusion. These persons, unlike paranoiacs, recognize that other people do not accept their own ideas concerning self-amputation. Symptoms are induced for the sake of becoming an amputee, and for the sake of erotic arousal, and seldom is self-injury repeated. The precise etiology of the condition is not known, and there is no agreed-upon method of treatment. —*quoted and adapted from documents written by John Money, PhD*

A Possible Chronology of Responsible Events from Early and Late Childhood:

—At **birth**: I am born with a moderately deformed right foot, which looks a bit like a knobby cluster of rotted oranges wrapped in soggy wet cardboard, and not like anything human. I see Polaroid images of the foot, images hidden in a small envelope in the bottom drawer of my father's bureau when I am twelve, and cry. They are trophies of his disdain for me. The foot causes me to walk funny, slightly leaning to my left side and shuffling unevenly forward. My father yells at me for walking funny, until I undergo surgery to fix my deformity at age fourteen. There is no mention of the clubbed foot thereafter.

—Domestic accident at **three years old**: When a boiling hot cast iron pot full of oatmeal capsizes from the stove, I am scalded on my right leg from the knee to the foot. It will take several months for this to heal, and I am rendered unable to walk (even poorly), for fourteen months.

—Near age **five**: Mom lights up a second cigar with a tiki torch from the backyard while she is mowing the lawn, and while dipping the torch down to her mouth for the light, spills propane fuel from the torch onto her leg, which immediately catches fire. She suffers third-degree burns and is bed-ridden for eight months.

—Ages **six** to **seventeen**: Mom begins answering all my calls, monitoring all my mail, and driving around in the car with the "mom seatbelt arm" on my chest at all times.

—Age **twelve**: I have my first thought that it might be nicer if I were a girl, the impulse of which I understand immediately to be overwhelmingly forbidden by my father. I transfer any and all trans-gender fantasies to my idea of a healthy limb removal. I break my leg on purpose when I force-fall off a horse at a pony riding carnival attraction, and enjoy the acts of cast, crutches, and the modified means of mobility.

—Age **thirteen**: My fascination with the apparatus of the guillotine as a machine of healing (and not of punishment) begins. I read many books on the subject, and attempt to make a miniature one of my own after a few months of research with small scraps of wood, a five-pound weight, and several razor blades. I only succeed in cutting off the most marginal amount of my left pinky finger, and feel dissatisfied with the process. Though the cut is small, I wear a band-aid with a tiny red bloodstain in the middle (shaped like a Peony flower) for months.

—Age **fifteen**: I find my father's shotgun in the laundry pantry inside the service porch, hidden behind several piles of clean old rags and a dust broom. I hold it, smell the raw wood of the stock, and aim it at my knee without pulling the trigger. I put it away, telling myself that I now know where it is when I need it.

Slack space between knowing who I am and exactly what needs to be done next, and then finding the wherewithal to get there. Slack space, colored gray. Gray is an underexploited space; this I have decided. Gray, the color of my world, seen through tiny slits when I crunch down my eyelids. Gray stands for impossible things: skyscrapers, entire cities, comic book gloom, stench. I am taking a shower. Dunking my head beneath the faucet, smoke smell from my hair rushes out into the wet space with me, musty like old luggage: the smell of gray space. I look down at my right leg. I am thinking about my video from the last time I watched it. Last night, I bound up the limb six inches above the knee with surgical tape and cyclone fencing tie wire, numbing the reddening band of skin on both sides of the tourniquet with Novocain that I stole from the dentist's office and several bags of frozen peas. There are bruises on the inside and outside of my thigh the color of eggplant, continuing down toward my calf in a shape that resembles the gulf coast of Florida. After nearly four hours, the pain was unbearable, practically impossible. The leg, hovering near rot, remains paranoid of what will happen next. Looking with fear in the direction of the healthy leg, the intact partner, it has no other choice. My video loops the 100-yard dash event at the Special Olympics. This is the hallmark of achievement in the face of adversity.

And then one day, a letter with no return address arrives...

To the rest of him, who faithfully remains intact,

I once overheard a wise man saying the following: "You don't know how to love the ones you love until they disappear abruptly."[1] With the passing of our union, now I know this to be indeed true. I need to tell you a few things; please indulge me for a paragraph or perhaps two...

I don't really know where to start. I have tried to sit down with this, beyond tears, in order to get somewhere using logic, tried to use something rooted in emotion, but also something that makes more sense out of the reality of the moment we are experiencing. Emotions usually run at a clip not nearly modest enough to allow a calm sincerity to

1   From: DeLilllo, Don. The Body Artist. New York: Scribner: 2001. Page 116.
     While others struggle with it, sharing is something we always took for granted. It was something we just did, the thing we were good at—you went, then I went.

guide one's thoughts and words. You must understand how much all of this has hurt me. I want to believe that this has little or nothing to do with you not wanting me: I know I have done nothing wrong, to be sure.

For several years, we have been together. There has been an acquired autopilot intensity to our shared commitment. Our physical separation now clarifies that situation as having ended, though remnants of what we had before still linger, and most likely, always will. Trust me, slowly I will get this all out. I am trying to understand that simply, our lives, once parallel, must have struck a gap. I know that resistance to what seems to have been the inevitable can only produce sadness and pain. To give in to pain will yield only suffering; *that*, I believe, is not necessary.

And so for the logic of it: I understand that there was a dire separation somewhere, likely induced by personal growth on your part, which led you to this point of cut-off, this endgame. I feel as though there is this truth: a person must become what he is, work on himself to the end, commit to one's destiny, follow through and be whole or compromise and be nothing; make one's mark on history if he so desires, or alternately relish the quiet that one can find. Do you see what I am talking about? I am telling you that I understand why this has happened. If I look at it through the memories of our past, I can see nothing but all the painful times we shared together, living as one body might live: completely. If I look at it through the plans we had made for our future together, all of those hopes I thought we once shared are dashed, grounded, no longer; there is only bitterness left. I must stay present in this. I dutifully remain loyal, with conviction, in this moment. I am hurt, but I know that you let me go because I was not what you needed; I couldn't begin to understand who you are without me, perhaps someone I wouldn't even recognize anymore.

Let this memory haunt you forever, and know that it is me who makes your stump itch,

Sincerely,

Ghost Leg

WE CONTROL THE PLOT AT DANGERSBY (HOW OUR RELATIONSHIP FALLS APART)

"Maybe there's a situation with the drain in there, like it's clogged." That melts away from me, more the slow speed of thinking out loud. I know he's probably wondering close to the same thing right now, so fixing things is really more the issue. When we get into it this deep, we tend to veer into metaphor. This is one of those times.

"You're sure we said everything drains off somewhere way down the hill—over there?" He's pointing off towards the freeway, away from us, which is north. Cars look tinier far in the distance, with their headlights starting to flicker on. The stray dogs somewhere in the same direction yip staccato simultaneously, and then do a moan-like thing that I can tell involves tilting their heads back and upwards, their long bodies casting jagged shadows down the edge of the hills in uneven angles. It sounds like there are two of them. "You know you hear things in a funny way, right? You know that about yourself, Jeanne? You think it's a girl thing?"

"It's almost six o'clock. Nothing's gonna get fixed tonight, obviously." For only a second, chilled winds bite the back of my neck, which is damp with sweat. It's nearly evening, but summer keeps it light 'til much later, making our situation seem hotter, somehow, more pointed. "Maybe we should just go get drinks. Blow it off some – for now.

Can you?" The radish I've been eating, well, more like gnawing on, has devolved to a tooth-sized chunk. Now it's gone. "So?"

"There's that 'hole in the wall' at the bottom of the hill. Seen it?" Sam looks right into my face every other time he says anything to me. It's been that way for the six months we've been doing this together. By "this," I mean "the project," which is what happened down in the basement again tonight.

It's another episode in our relationship. We've just moved into the phase where I can no longer count how many times they've happened, the physical parts, and I'm realizing exactly that, now. I look over at him, then at the freeway again. There isn't really any basement. It's still part of the metaphor we've developed, this thing that exists between us like a third person in our relationship; between us is a story about a coroner. "You wanna just go there? It's close."

Most of Sam's girlfriends have been young, nearly too young; he says it's just been easier that way. He doesn't do much that's "easier," but this is one thing he's apparently excused himself about. So here I am, with some questions that won't seem to go away. That part of Sam's contribution to our relationship—meaning his past, well—it weirded me out the first time he talked about it, if I am perfectly honest with myself. Maybe there's always been a problem I've just refused to pay complete attention to.

"Yeah," he says half-heartedly. "Sounds good. I like it best when you give in."

"I pressed pause." I'm usually the one in control here, the author of our twisted little tale, and not because the whole thing with us and our story about the coroner started out as my idea, but because I need to be in control. "I didn't give in, I mean." Our main character, he rents a house in the hills, secluded and lonely, practices some sadistic and unholy shit until he and whoever else either gets caught or bored or both. They use the basement to clean up everything afterwards.

That's the story. Our story—the story of us. I don't really mean that, but sometimes—it's exactly what this feels like. So far, everything's going according to plan, I guess. If you can push the metaphor around enough, that is. "Let's go there. Now." That came out more forceful than I thought it would.

Either way, we're going there now, to the bar. I think we both need a break, and cold beer tends to cleanse more than just the palate. This is a truth upon which each of us has come to rely.

§ § §

We sit in the bar. Most of what happens here in this city writes itself out like a fiction and then, shortly after, falls apart. I named our character's rented house Dangersby, which to me sounds better, or maybe just more regal, when you say it with a British accent. *Dangersby.* Our guy lives in a house with a name.

I don't know what came first: if things started to sour a little bit with Sam or if I got this fucked up idea for "the project" in my head. Like maybe it was all just my imagination, but I guess that could go either way, too. I wonder now if he's changed too, or if he even notices how he's different than he was at the beginning—or if it's really just that he's always been the same and now I'm noticing different things about him that seem impenetrable, ugly and distant. Maybe we never existed and I'm just some maniac, and everything like this goes all awry whenever I'm involved, or else none of the bodies in our story ever showed up in the basement at Dangersby at all, and I'm just on vacation from my life, and reality, relationships and everyone else. It doesn't matter now, really at all, I think. Tonight our story's character cuts open the sixth, maybe the seventh body. It's a girl.

We've discussed this before, Sam and me, some time after the second episode in our story together. This time, it comes out of me like this: "I think that he has this ability to pick a body apart, to identify and describe each element as it exists independent of anything else it might be attached to." The best part about this was that we could talk about ourselves without really talking about ourselves. Then our guy started to take on a life of his own—our character, the coroner, became an independent entity living up there in make-believe land at Dangersby.

"You mean, like—it's a kind of detachment he uses?" Sam responds; his big thing is playing along. He puts it on display to almost everyone, like he's gonna play harder than anyone else, and make sure they know it. "To numb himself when things get too difficult, emotionally speaking—like that?"

Bodies make more sense to me when things are disconnected, unique and named. So maybe this thought that I've had before has seeped into our make-believe. Our character owns a part of it too—it's his idea, as well. Now when we write our story, it's more like dreaming, when a person's head tries to clean house during the night, kind of based on whatever shit they've seen that day. "There are ears in the world right now that this guy's fallen in love with, though I am sure they don't know it," I say.

Sam's curiosity is stirred, and he sinks his teeth in a bit deeper. I used to love this about him. Now, it just confuses me. "He could nibble and lick information off them until they melted down to half their original size." I see the saliva building up in his mouth when he licks his lips between lines. "It's been that way for as long as he can remember. But he's never told anyone, though." He's sitting on the edge of his barstool now, upright and stiff. Something in him is still missing in us, or maybe it's just the part I'm starting to realize I'll never be able to get to—something refusing to be named.

There's nothing apologetic about this fascination, about breaking down the human equation to smaller, easier-to-handle elements. It's something I'm not sure I should apologize about. "He only does it when he has to. When things get so impossible it makes him see crooked." This is my thing now—I think I've just always had more to be confused about than Sam has, and now Sam's a big part of that confusion. I've offered him this as a sort of apology: "That's the only way he can describe it, even when he's looking straight ahead at nothing, or at the craggy, snarled oak tree perched in his front lawn." Now he knows it's about me. When our story dips back into what's real, like the tree, Sam gets scared.

He first said he liked me mostly for my mouth, which is slightly crooked, sloping down and to the left when a person looks at me straight on. Of course, I think this is funny because his lips are swollen, purpley, with freckles dotting patterns down and over his nose right up to them. And it was those lips that puffed up fiercely whenever he got angry, which was often, so I'm not sure what gives him the right to make a big deal out of my mouth.

Sam has never met many of my friends, and I think it's better that way, because I know that none of them would ever have gotten along, or else they would have gotten along way too well for me to handle. I like it better when different people in my life stay in the private compartments I make for them. Controlled and fixed, they tend to do less damage than when I introduce them to each other and weird social overlaps occur. This helps to keep things organized. It's no wonder our main character is a coroner. After all, how much damage can a dead person do, and more importantly, how much more can a dead person get damaged? The whole thing's ultimately about organization for our guy.

§ § §

The first time I met Sam was at a bar in the neighborhood; a mutual acquaintance had set us up. He sat next to me for several moments without saying anything, and I thought that somehow, maybe, he was from out of town. Not like he was wearing cowboy boots and dungarees or anything; it was way more subtle than that. Things just tend to fit in and make a kind of sense around here. Sam didn't.

"I lost my parents." This was the first thing he ever said to me. I figured he was maybe on vacation or something when it happened. He looked barely mid-twenties, though I found out later he was closer to thirty, about six years older than me. The baby blue t-shirt he wore said "I'm Retired (but I work part time spoiling my grandkids)" in a dirt-brown script across the front. Turns out he was making a joke – his parents were never lost, or dead, or anything else. They were just there – watching television or something, in the house where he had grown up. It was exactly that kind of detail that bothered me now, though in the beginning I was fascinated.

§ § §

There's a lapse in our story now, and Sam has slumped down into his chair again. This is when it gets hard. "Tell me how it looks again when he goes inside." Maybe I try to sound disinterested. There's a television in the bar that's directly in my line of vision. I'm staring at an image of a ship that is somehow on fire, out in the middle of the ocean, sinking impossibly into the deep water, crawling with passengers who are squirming around on its decks and each other. One never thinks these things can happen.

"I thought maybe, somehow, that you could be trusted," he says. I already knew Sam had nothing to lose; he was *that* guy. No one to answer to for whatever shit he might possibly get himself into, and worse—proud of it. The basement in our story is the place he goes when it gets like this. I made it that way for him, a gesture meant to make things better. The isolation up in the hills, that was all him. I'm not sure whose gifts are better. There is no one else around us, and so we keep on drinking.

When I finally get Sam to open up again, it's through our guy. He's given in this time, and I get to hear my favorite part. This might be the beer talking. "She was standing near the bus stop at the bottom of the long hill that leads to Dangersby. He circles around the block, leaving the girl standing there on the small sidewalk of dirt, not going anywhere. He pulls over, and she gets in without saying a word." In our story, this was as easy as things ever got. He seems tired, but I think it's an act.

I already know that in the basement of our story, there are no windows. Sam made that part happen. It probably made him feel like he could talk about stuff that way, with no one watching our guy. Everything but the instruments and the stainless steel tables down there assumes a tone close to a washed-out gray blue. I'm imagining the details in my head as Sam's telling the part about how at Dangersby, in our story, the coroner's turned his basement into a morgue of sorts, where he can examine the bodies he drags down there.

The walls are tiled, as is the floor and ceiling, with small, six-inch squares and a deep black grout, which never appears soiled. At regular intervals along the walls and three feet up from the floor, there are a dozen electrical boxes, poking out into the room like small square eyes. Water spigots jut out here and there, angled down toward the floor.

In the center of everything on the ground there is a large (by which I mean nearly a foot wide) stainless steel drain, that has even slats separated by half an inch of open space, looking down into the ground several unlit feet beneath the floor itself. This is all perfectly fine, though, because as our metaphor, the story of us, it makes sense. Somehow, we were meant to become a bottomless hole. Now I'm trying to remember if I decided that I was that drip, or if what really mattered was that we were cutting up bodies in our story. This is another part of the confusion. Everything on the tiled floor slopes imperceptibly toward this drain.

"There is the tiny, omnipresent sound of running water slowly heading downward. The basement air smells heavy and sterile, like bleach," Sam whispers. He crawls into parts of the story, almost. It's like he's a quiet fly on the basement wall, and he's really watching as he's telling me what our guy's doing.

"There are two sinks, side by side. The door to the basement is steel, solid, and always stays locked." I usually add this part. Beyond control, I'm thinking about safety and how we're maybe more like those sinks. Functional, purposeful and always side by side. But we both know that's not the case. We may be nearing our end.

Fluorescent light fixtures hanging tightly, too close to the ceiling, buzz and drop light in wide, even shapes down on our guy, the coroner. Arranged in long rows on the tables along the west wall of the basement, the surgical tools, mostly anodized black aluminum or stainless steel, resemble rows of carnivorous dinosaur teeth, jagged and precise, curved and ominous. "In the basement, he covers his shoes in rubber boots, twice the size of his feet; one thing is consistent down here: there's always a lot of blood." This doesn't come out of him with any sort of mock-ghoulishness. He's completely sincere, which for a second, catches me off-guard. I'm thinking maybe I'm wrong about us. Maybe we can still work out something together—like our story doesn't actually end soon. Only no one talks in the basement at Dangersby. The basement is for paying attention. It's a purely visual experience. We watch ourselves happen to each other in the story we write together. And we both know where this is going.

"He wants to understand the body. He wants to look into it, to see what it feels like, to understand beyond the pinks inside his mouth or the reds and whites of his eyeballs, what colors and textures exist in there." Sam's messages are confusing to me. I don't know what to think when he's this careful with our story, or when he makes our guy so curious. It's not his style. Sam's always been a take-it-or-leave-it kind of person, so him acting like we've got a choice in the matter is strange. "There seems an endless amount of information, an absurd amount of detail to consider, and he wanted to know all of it. Then, as he learned more, he liked it more."

Sam's watching our guy work. He's already finished his second beer, and decided not to order anything else tonight. The girl's naked, lying on her back on the table in the basement. She's been dead for only a couple of hours. She's never seen the basement at Dangersby. I'm about to look inside of her for the first time. This is the first time things have gotten this bad. This is where I have to take control.

"The scalpel is too sharp, cuts more than he wants it to most of the time, so he has to be careful to make quick, focused motions with it, holding onto it like a pen or a pencil." The tools know what to do on their own, it seems. All of this with Sam was easy at first. He was playful and I was—thinking I was less confused than I always am. We found a brief moment at the same time we found each other, and that's when our story started. "Holding open a flap of skin on the chest with two fingers curled under and now slipping a bit inside, he splits the body open like a wet paper bag as his fingers trail down behind the blade, which is heading south, down from her throat. Beneath her skin, maybe half an inch below, yellowy and flaccid cauliflower-shaped globs of spongy fat and tissue bubble up, spill out onto the ribs and then onto the table." I'm not even looking at Sam anymore. This part of the story is mine, and I want him to get the point. "Working his hands further and further down into the body, gurgling noises and the sound of running water. The sensation of warm fluids on his rubber gloves, a pale pink."

"I want this part." Sam's brought the argument full circle now, and I let him have it, feeling something shift, release in me. "He's into the main cavity of the torso up to his elbow, his hands dancing around inside in sloppy, drunken ballet-like half circles, trying to figure something out." Sam's not much for poetry, but when he's angry, or scared, it's different. Maybe he's really given up, so it's someone else's story he's telling now, which makes it easier for him. "He cuts out a lung, which he has to get hold of firmly and pull up on, until something suddenly dislodges, and the organ hangs there over the chest in his hand like some kind of uprooted tree stump, viscous and bloody, practically alive itself."

I'm finding it harder to breathe now, but I handed our guy off to Sam so him reaching back in for more is only fair. "This is the tongue, which is longer than one might imagine, hanging there from the inside of the throat like a soft pink strand of meat. Grisly is the only word to describe what's going on here." I don't have much else to say. Our guy suddenly goes quiet.

Sam and I are completely engaged with this body, whose ribcage is now spread wide, the yellowed bones spotted with blood, drying and clotted, looking more like grilled slices of eggplant than anything else. Looking down at his feet, the character has to notice fluids building up on the tiled floor. The drain is covered with small chunks of flesh and jagged strips of bone, other small organs floating over it. Everything is going down, or trying to, at least. It all devolves.

The body lies there on the table, entirely opened up in front of us, not moving for anything or anyone until we decide exactly what happens next. And maybe that's when it all falls apart.

LETTER TO MY EX-WIFE, IN NEED OF AN EXPLANATION

Dear Boo-Boo,

I am guessing you have been wondering where I went to lately, given the fact that I haven't been home for a while. So—I am staying with a friend for now, somewhere in the neighborhood, actually, but don't try to find me or anything. I will be looking for my own apartment soon, so don't worry about my accommodations. Hey! I just realized this is really the first time I've written you a letter! I mean, there were of course the little love notes in the beginning, but that was so long ago. Just so you know, I will never be coming home again, and I thought that maybe I would tell you why. I've evolved! Oh my God, finally—I've become someone more complete, almost entirely fulfilled now, so changed that our friends who knew me before might not even recognize me anymore. But I'm proud, really—so no freak-outs, please. Plus, because the things that have currently taken hold of my attention are relatively new for me, I thought that this letter might give me a chance to put down in ink some ideas about why I have taken such a fancy to my new hobbies. Since you haven't seen or heard from me in about a month, you have to be wondering what the heck happened. Furthermore, because we didn't have sex for the last sixty-four days of our relationship (and I know how you feel about such lapses in what you currently refer to as "momma's little ham glazing sessions"), I am guessing that matters have been greatly complicated in your mind. I know the tendencies of your imagination quite well, what with all those evil gnomes of self-destruction pushing their nubby little fingers around in your cerebral cortex, conjuring up the most unholy of thoughts. After all, I would want and expect the same from you, where explanations are concerned. We did love each other, in my estimation. Maybe you actually even still do! We cut each other's toenails, for chrissake. How much closer to someone can you be?

Now then. The point of this letter. Ok, here goes… a curious event took place some weeks ago, which, I believe, has changed me forever. I'm still grappling with the specifics of this event myself. To launch into things straight away, I think, could only upset and perhaps even terrify you, but I am going to do it like that anyway. You always said, "Rip the band-aid off quickly, don't snail it off!" I thought that was so cute, with the thing about the snail and how they're practically the same color as the band-aids, and then they move so slowly along, the snails that is, taking like *a year* just to make it from the driveway to the edge of the flower pots with the sweet-smelling gardenias on our front porch. I'll really miss that sense of humor you've got, won't I! And remember the time when you accidentally stepped on that snail, crunching it beneath your bare foot as you hopped high trying to avoid it with slippers in your hand? The one in the front of the long line of them, heading towards the porch? So clumsy you always were! Endearing, to say the least. I even stepped on one that night too – just to be supportive! But now I think I may be digressing.

Deep breath.

So there was this apparently long-standing joke going on between certain unnamed co-workers of mine down at the dental office. (Those straight white coats we all wear don't necessarily signify anything about *mental* hygiene). So the joke goes like this: a dentist leaves the office around lunchtime (this time it was Dr. Greenberg), much in the same manner as he would any other day of the week. About two hours later, he calls up the office answering service, and in a feverish manner, leaves an out-of-breath message for a specific dentist (this time, me). The terms of the joke are brief: pick a dentist who is not in on the joke yet, and be as quick as possible in order to heighten the effect. Can you see where this is going, Honey? You always said I was so gullible! You had no idea the extent to which you were right about that! All that was left on the message: a telephone number, the feeling of an extraordinary amount of concern and danger, and the plain fact that the dentist leaving the message was apparently in a great deal of trouble. Several minutes later, I was called out of a routine scraping and cleaning session with Mrs. Beecker, that cute old German lady with the mauve-colored hair who we always see at the video store spying on the patrons behind the saloon doors that close off the porno section of the store. You know Mrs. Beecker? Sure you do. Anyway, so

I got the message, scribbled down the telephone number and immediately called up, frantic, wondering if a bail bondsman or an emergency room nurse would pick up the other end of the line.

Instead, this was the message that I heard. I wrote it down word for word, even though I had to call the number ten or fifteen times that day to do it. You know how bad you always said my memory was, especially for important things like our anniversary! Here was what the voice said on the machine:

"Hello and welcome to the information line for the L.A. Jacks, where you, too, may see the thing itself. The L.A. Jacks is a group of men who like to jack off with like-minded men. Neither a business nor a religion, we are a public service organization now in our nineteenth year. We meet twice a month on the 2nd and 4th Monday; doors open at 7:30pm and close promptly at 8:30. Don't be late. This month, we meet on the 12th and the 26th. Our location is 1601 Hope, downtown at the Friction Booth. Our rules are simple. Mandatory clothes check. J-O play only. No cock sucking, no butthole play. No obnoxious behavior. No poppers, for example. Don't be shy, smile and have fun. We ask a contribution of seven dollars. You may bring beverages in cans. We provide the lube and paper towels. Fetish wear is welcome. Creative pecker play and group scenes are highly encouraged. So come on down! Join L.A. Jacks for an evening of poetry in motion, where you too may see the thing itself."

Needless to say, I was a bit confused. I mean, Honey—
come on! What would you have thought? You know I'm
not always the quickest on the uptake when faced with
long, drawn-out explanations of things I know nothing
about, like that time you tried to explain to me what soap
operas were, and why they were so important. I was so lost!
My brain felt like it turned into mashed potatoes—and I
think you even said as much, judging by the look on my
face. Well—this time the same sort of thing happened, I
guess. I wasn't really confused about what had gone wrong
with Dr. Greenberg (if there was even anything at all), but
more along the lines of exactly what would be considered
"obnoxious behavior" in such an environment as was
described over the telephone and, further, what the exact
nature of "creative pecker play" might be. Dr. Greenberg
and the others in the office had a tremendous laugh at my
expense, and I played the part of the jackass they needed
to get the most out of their gag. You would have cried if
you had seen how sad I pretended to be! It was terrible,
in a way, I suppose. In reality, I had already decided that I
was going to go and check out the Jacks. I mean, why not?
Wasn't it you, Dear, who always encouraged me to be a
little bit more experimental? I mean, of course, you were
mostly talking about getting a bit deeper into the menus of
the restaurants we'd have dinner in, given my propensity
for always ordering the same dishes. But this was real!
You'd have been so proud of your brave little boy!

For several weeks afterward, I came home on my
lunch breaks, and while you were at work at the Baklava

Warehouse over in Glendale, I practiced new and (what I thought would be) complicated methods of "creative pecker play" there in front of our bedroom mirror, by myself.

I developed a technique of performing a "Three Stooges" -like scenario around my penis, in much the same manner as they chased each other around a couch, with the penis acting as Curly, my balls playing Larry and my right hand as Moe—obviously. We both used to laugh at how mean he could be to his brothers! Wait—were they his brothers? Now I can't remember. You were always the one who could clear up such mysteries. Oh well. I was impressed with my own apparent brilliance, to say the least, having devised such play-acting rituals. Truly "creative," wouldn't you agree? I did the "wubwubwubwub" that so often came out in the frenetic falsetto from the high-strung Curly directly before receiving a beating from Moe. I lifted my balls up either inside my inguinal canal or up and under my legs where I would tuck them in between my butt cheeks. Larry was always the scared but calm one who seemed to be able to get away from Moe, so it made perfect sense to me to hide my balls. When I did the reverse tuck (which I opted for most of the time), I would turn around and bend over to see what it looked like in the mirror, and decided to call this Part 2 section of my pecker play "Oops I sat in hairy gum!" Back to the Stooges. I'm so bad at staying focused! Aarrgh! You were right about that, Sweetheart. And I'm sorry. But what really worked about my act, if you want to know the truth, was the labored "Why You" that I started just like Moe from the side of my mouth right as I began flogging my penis with all the confidence of a toilet plunger in a plumbing factory. I mean, real confidently. For the grand finale, I would hum the ending notes of the Stooges theme song, emitting a steadily timed stream of semen onto the mirror, ending with the "da da da duh—da duh." You know the song I mean, Honey—it was always your cue to get up and use the bathroom on those late Saturday mornings when we'd stay in bed watching tv.

Sometime soon after that, I decided I was ready. I tucked a couple of cans of Old Milwaukee into my leather coat and went down to the Friction Booth. I didn't recognize anyone there at first, but soon enough I noticed that the cook from the House of Pancakes (the one we ate in last June every weekend when we had the kitchen re-done) was there. What was his name? I forget. He must have come directly from IHOP because he still had that floppy white hat on with the "Rooty Tooty Fresh and Fruity" button flair pinned to it. *And* Mr. Hilton from those bird painting classes you took down at the park was there. He took a while to register in my head, but then I remembered the Baltimore Orioles baseball cap he always wore, and when he took it off later on during the session to launch his entire load right into it, I realized it was indeed him. He didn't spill a drop or anything! You would have been so impressed because, if I recall correctly, you always used to come home from that class and tell me stories about how the old guy would consistently spill his paint jars on the floor. So strange, how sometimes you can be so wrong, and other times, you can't help but get it right. Right as he put the cap back on, I saw some white jizz dribble down his left temple as the wet stain began to seep through the black space behind the bird. I thought for a second that it looked like the bird had taken a shit on his head! But that's going too far, I suppose. He didn't care either way, though—he just brushed the goo back into his sideburns and behind his ear, readjusting his cap pretty much the same way Cal Ripken did in every game he ever played. And I know you know what I mean! Aren't you glad now that I made you sit through so many baseball games? Otherwise, you'd have no idea what I was just referring to.

So, yes—it was a little weird being in the same room with a bunch of guys, standing around in a lazy circle (about two or three players deep), stroking off in roughly concentric circles like so many rows of shark teeth. Not gay, or anything, though. Weird, right? 'Cause you'd kinda have to imagine it would be, but it wasn't. *At all.* I don't know about creative, but as far as I could tell, the Three Stooges thing went over pretty big-time. Right when I did the Curly laugh and tucked Larry in between my butt cheeks, I got a few pats on the back from a couple of the guys standing nearby. I could swear the hollering that sounded like wild Amazonian birds emanating from the shadows on the other side of the room—those were for me, too, I think. Seriously! Then I guess I went too far, or else I just misunderstood the part about no butthole play, 'cause I had originally thought that they meant *just don't play with anyone else's butthole.* I didn't realize they actually meant *don't play with any butthole in the entire room,* **including your own butthole**. When I turned around, Honey, and bent over with my ass facing the middle of the circle, thinking I was gearing up to a grander finale after I had my first release, I must have gotten a little carried away. I don't know what kind of weird confidence swept over me, but it was like getting hit in the face by a chilly Chicago wind or something, because it was powerful. For no reason at all, I stuck my thumb up my butt to further highlight the "Oops I just sat in hairy gum" visual. I hadn't even practiced that part at the house, so I probably should have been more nervous about it anyway. But there I was, Sweetheart—bein' all spontaneous, just like you always wished for me to be! I really did it, too! The next thing I know, I am being rather hastily (and somewhat awkwardly) rushed out through the two rows of guys behind me and toward the dressing rooms. I remembered the gentleman escorting me out was the self-proclaimed Master of Ceremonies who had announced, "Let the jack-offery begin!" around half past eight, just after they shut and locked the front doors. He had really hairy hands and his thumbs were cranked into my torso as he pulled me out of the group. He was so rough! I had bruises like from a seatbelt when you get in a car wreck. Back in the entry room of the club, I was rudely handed my clothes when the Master, addressing me in short, angry lines, asked me to please go ahead and take at least a few weeks off before I made another appearance at the Jacks. He said he was intrigued, even impressed with my routine, but in the end, he had to make sure to look out for the more shy members of the club. Apparently, in his

43

wisdom and experience with the Jacks, he figured that my high level of showmanship might actually be off-putting to some of the membership, and figured they'd be able to forgive and forget after a little while, just give them a chance by taking some time off. That was embarrassing, but also kinda nice to finally be singled out for something. Weird, right? I'm sure you can see through all that, and find some way to be proud of me for putting myself out there so much.

More to the point, I had overheard some guys talking about something called "back ache" or "bake-off" or something like that, and I asked them about it during the pre-festivities in the locker room, and they said they would give me a number a little bit later. When I got home that night, I realized that when I bent over to do the trick with Larry from the Three Stooges, one of those guys must have been standing next to me (it was kind of dark, like I told you before). He had surreptitiously tucked a business card into the boots I was wearing with the phone number that he had mentioned earlier. Most of the guys at Jacks left their shoes on too, or at the very least their socks, so no—I didn't feel weird about that at the time at all. And thank God, anyway, because I don't know where he would have put the business card had I taken my shoes and socks off in the first place! I guess sometimes it really pays off to be such a practical thinker. Right, Honey?

The card said "Bukkake Focus Group" in a very straightforward all caps font, and only had a phone number with an area code for somewhere in the middle of Los

Angeles. I took the card home, and the next day at work started doing a little research on the Internet in between fillings and cleanings. It was easy to see why I had thought they were talking about a "back ache," or whatever it was I thought I heard them saying. When I tried typing "bukkake" into the search engine, "back ache" was what it thought I was asking for, and all the search turned up was a bunch of local chiropractors and back pain specialists. Eventually I refined my search enough to figure out what was going on with the Focus Group whose card announced them so professionally. The recent cultural phenomenon that I discovered through this research needs a bit of explaining. Hey—if I didn't know what it was, then there's no way in heck that you would! And what good would this letter do for either of us if I didn't make my new situation clear to both of us?

Bukkake, just so you know, is from Japan. You've always been pretty good with the cultural origins of words, so maybe you could have guessed this. Though the term bukkake is not a sexual term at all, it has been used to dub what stands as the premier, hot fetish racing through the world at the moment. Grammatically, bukkake in Japanese is the base form of a verb, yet as it stands alone, it is a noun that means "splash," or "heavy squirt." All sexual connotations aside, it stands as a pretty normal word in the Japanese language, from what I can tell. Japan even has a soup called "bukkake udon," it's so normal over there. I guess the soup has nothing to do with sex at all; it's just called bukkake because they think it makes the soup sound more appetizing. They put a lot of vegetables and liquid in the soup, and by calling it bukkake, they believe it gives the feeling that the soup was made quickly and with more freshness, like someone just "splashed" the soup together. I thought that was so interesting when I read it the first time! Don't you think so?

Here's how the history of the *sexual* term "bukkake" goes. Around the late eighties and early nineties, a couple of Japanese video companies were trying to make videos that catered to facial and sperm lovers in Japan. (In case you didn't know, a "facial" is a term in pornography that means "to launch a jack-off spray onto the face of the other party or parties participating in the sexual act." You know how much I have always been very sensitive, and very into public displays of affection like holding hands, kissing or walking arm in arm? This seemed so sweet to me when I read about it. You know – it was like a kind of affectionate display, taken to a brand new extreme!) So anyway, companies like "Soft on Demand," "Shuttle Cocks & Badminton Girls," "Madame Woo's Enormous Genitals Video Group," "Deeps" and a few other smaller ones decided to make videos that would consist of a single girl getting facial after facial, over and over again—like a fire that just couldn't be put out. It's really kind of loving, in a way, if you let yourself think about it in a poetic light. Like a perverse, acted-out Hallmark card of pornography. It's just like the time right after two people get married, and everyone at the wedding throws handfuls of rice onto them as they attempt to make their getaway in a limousine out in front of the church. Just hurling love at the couple, all the love you have to give at that very moment. Remember when they did that to us? We thought we had it made, forever. Didn't we?

Anyway, you can do research on the Internet if you want to. I'll give you a little tip on a site called "NativityBukkake.com," where a Japanese video company has mapped out plans for a new release next fall. In this themed bukkake series, it seems that American guest director Flynn Flin has decided that, right in time for the holidays next year, he would retell the greatest story ever told by man: the story of the birth of the savior. His idea is to recreate historic Bethlehem, complete with straw and donkeys and chickens and everything, and have the bukkake sequence all take place around a stable with live cattle. I'm probably going to hell for just writing down the sacrilegious plot in this letter to you, so I can't imagine where Flynn Flin is headed after he dies! There would be at least 150 guys dressed up in costumes like the three kings, Mary and Joseph, the Inn Keeper and the shepherd, and the recipient would be resting in the small manger in the center of the stable, dressed in swaddling white robes with just her sweet little Japanese face showing. Amazing. You should really take a look if you get a second.

So bottom line, Honey, I called the number on the card. The Bukkake Focus Group meets next Tuesday, and since I've been temporarily banned from the Jacks, I figure I might as well go and check it out. I hope you are well and not missing me too much. You always did really great things around the house those times when dental conferences would call me out of town for the weekend, and you'd be by yourself for a couple of days, reading or knitting or rearranging the furniture in the living room. Maybe we can meet up for tea or coffee or even a glass of wine when this whole thing blows over a little bit. I am sure you need your space right now too, and both of us need a little time to let all this stuff sink in. Who knows what I've uncovered for myself with all this public love business, but just trust that maybe I'm as well as I've really ever been.

Warm regards,

Mitch

A BRIEF HISTORY OF THE TUPPERWARE PARTY

You think about it all the time. The phrase all the time should be expanded upon. *All the time* means *every second of every day since you first met her.* You are just a shade over six feet tall, and every square inch of real estate on your body is covered in coarse, tightly curled, low-lying black hair. Your girlfriend: small, baby-like. You are bear-man reincarnate, mistaken (possibly not enough) for Sasquatch. You wonder: how could she really love you, for you are closer to her pet than her husband? If sighted from behind, she could be your twelve-year-old daughter walking along beside you, a "tween" with her ultimate protector. It's raining again for the fourteenth day in a row. You know because you've been counting. It's become a regular thing for you. Day one: raining. Day two, raining, and so forth. You wake up, count the next consecutive day of rain pleasantly disturbing you from outside the bedroom window over the bed, then hook the bathrobe onto your arm from over the bathroom door. A gorilla dismounting the stage and returning to the dressing room after a Vegas lounge act. Next: puddle-step down the driveway to retrieve the newspaper from its wet little spot on the ground. They never include this moment in the "let's all stop and give thanks for how important plastic has become in our lives" commercials. Pausing in front of the little plastic sack protecting the dry newspaper at your feet, you wonder, why not? Good newspaper boy. You bounce in through the front door, dampened fur and all, dripping from thousands of tiny, hairy ringlets, suddenly troubled by a nagging voice somewhere in your mind. What was that thing you were supposed to attend to today? Shedding your slippers, you smell fresh coffee brewing, and the thought is gone. The tiny love goddess has arisen.

Naked, she resembles a small white tree freshly stripped of its bark. (You imagine yourself a giant old oak with misshapen limbs, covered everywhere in thick, damp moss and lichen, medieval-style.) She is standing in the kitchen, wearing the bubble-gum pink terri-cloth robe you gave her for Christmas last year, the one you both joked about. You want so badly to be accepted by her, taken in as her equal, two matching parts that somehow belong to the world in your togetherness. And oh, how the puffy edges of hot pink fuzz on that robe make her look like a miniature show poodle in action. Mental flash—Christmas morning, she: perched on all fours, barking shrill whelps from atop the bed, new pink robe folded back to reveal soft white butt flesh the exact color of chamomile tea with milk in it; you: stunned at first, then, rolling around on the bedroom floor in a fit of hysteria, laughing so hard that day, there was blood in your pee that night before bed.

The kitchen counter-top, which she now stands in front of, is shaped in a horseshoe, curved around her like the letter "U." With both her hands perched on the smooth gray tile, palms face-down, elbows turned outward with finger tips pointing into the middle, she stands there. You can see from over her shoulder that they form a shape resembling an object the size of a small white envelope. You imagine yourself a tiny, crisp white sheet of paper with only the words *I am your perfect other* scrawled upon it, folded neatly and tucked inside that envelope of her—yet in reality, you know this is a thing you'll never be. Instead, you are a two hundred and forty-seven pound mammoth (most of the time). She is only a shade over five feet tall, barely one hundred pounds, and completely hairless. (*Little baby,* you coo, mumbling to yourself.) This is not normal, you think. Mating pairs of humans should be roughly equal in size, shouldn't they? That's what all the textbooks said in grade school. You recall picture after picture of other mammals in pairs, nestled in tightly, side by side, one looking roughly like a medium, and the other a bit closer to a *large*, were you to be comparing t-shirts or containers of milk. They should at least be covered in the same amount of mammal hair, yes? After all, you have never seen a grizzly bear snuggling up next to a naked mole rat. Moreover, when the large and the small are bred together, as in the dog kingdom, weird deformities and aberrations occur, the dysfunctional spawn growing ears more appropriate for bats, spots as on cows, or jaw bones with the sheer power of a hippo's. This line of questioning will get you nowhere, but it is your constant temptation to lapse into self-hatred and masochism. How deeply you feel the need to be loved by her, to be accepted completely, even in your grotesque and loathsome form. You feel your hair growing longer even as you think these words to yourself. You are becoming, all the time, more of what you know she can't possibly love. This much you know. Bad doggie!

She holds a steaming cup of coffee out to you, standing before you on the cream and pumpkin colored linoleum kitchen floor. One day, you will have your way and will convince her to change the color to a dark root-beer brown, which will discretely hide the evidence of your shedding, which, in a day or two, can turn the linoleum into what appears to be a well-worn and heavily matted fur rug, upon anyone's close inspection. Humbly, you accept the coffee. Once her hand is emptied of the cup, she uses it to scumble around in the damp hair inside your robe, which has opened subtly in a curved V-shape around your burly neck, only to reveal the black mass of still-damp hair lying there. Her hand looks like a toddler's fist on a giant black sheep dog's belly. You know this to be true, and her scrubbing motion, though it lasts for only a few seconds, does nothing to refute or deny the analogy. *Good doggie*, she is saying, *Good doggie!* Inside, you are half-purring.

It's Sunday. Day fourteen in the rain count, the biblical nature of which is not lost on you. Morning hurriedly becomes late morning, which gives way to afternoon, with considerably more urgency. Three in the afternoon, to be exact. You've done your best to cover yourself in human clothes; ones that provide your hairiness ample room to breathe and grow, which means you're wearing loose-fitting white linen pants and a baggy button-up pale blue over-shirt. With a pronounced knock-knock at the front door, you suddenly remember why you've had that nagging little voice inside your head all morning. Your soon-to-be father-in-law has come for Sunday dinner.

It's still raining outside. If the beating of rain could be registered at a volume of three before you opened the door, then once you've got it open to receive your guest, it's something closer to an eight or nine on the volume dial and overpowering enough to drown out all conversation. Yelling in his direction and motioning dramatically with both of your shaggy bear arms, you encourage him to fold up the umbrella outside, and not inside (as it is bad luck to bring open umbrellas inside the house). You intend to remind him in a much calmer manner once the door has been closed again. Disregarding your advice, the old man rumbles in through the front door with the open umbrella. You snag it from him and bobble the clumsy thing for a few seconds before you manage to close it back up. The umbrella: an amazing yet awkward invention. It's been the same since the first day it was made. The old man smells like bacon again today, maybe his only endearing quality. But bacon to a bear is like the Holy Grail of dinner bells. This is a man you could easily take down. You try, if only for a second, to remember how much room is left in your freezer and realize you haven't been in there for a long while. If only the box was empty, you are certain you could store the uneaten limbs for the several weeks it might take to finish him off completely. You quickly reprimand yourself for such a thought, and return to the moment there in the entry hall. The little girl offers a tiny "Hi Dad" from the kitchen where she is deep in the meal preparation, simmering, chopping and slicing things for supper. You acknowledge this greeting to yourself, evidence of the closeness of their connection, a thing you most likely will never have with her. Of equal importance, you think maybe you will be visited by only a stroke or two of bad luck now. Perhaps you caught the whole umbrella-in-the-house bad luck deal just in time. You're sure it's been done before; people walk underneath a leaning step-ladder in public all the time, halting sharply halfway to retreat back out and around the ladder they nearly bolted under. A clean save, to be sure. Bad luck, you believe, like jams, jellies and even slain grizzly bears, can be preserved for use at a later time.

You retire to the living room, where you gracefully concede your favorite chair, opting for the couch instead. *Why not?* You think to yourself. The couch is nice too, and how often is the family dog allowed, even encouraged, to sit on the couch? You bought it, didn't you? Total silence ensues. What must she be thinking in the kitchen? She knows better than anyone that you don't get along with him: you've both watched the programs on the children who shoot their parents dead. Step-parents can get shot, too. No one is immune to death by bullet. Not even the old man. And he's the one person in the world who represents the position you'd like to be in: unconditionally accepted by her. What that must be like! You examine him closely, struggling like a scientist to locate his imperfections, to bring his ugliness out into the open, to make yourself feel like you've got even just half a chance to be loved. Instead, you feel itchy. Itchy on the back, itchy on the legs, itchy in the crotch. The hair, it has a mind of its own, and grows beneath your clothes at a speed that would register to the human eye, were someone to watch it closely enough. You sit there grinding out the scratches in a V-motion up and down either side of your groin, determined to be thorough, yet secretive. "So—" you say in the old man's direction, not really looking at him, merely a formality. Itchy gorilla man watching television with old man, beautiful hairless baby in the kitchen cooking dinner. This is the scene in your house now.

You hate football, but here is an occasion where you can find it excusable. No conversation required with the old man for at least two or three hours. All of your senses are busy for the moment. Two eyes alternate from the television in front of you to the kitchen behind you. The old man is wearing fashionable corduroy slacks and a heavy knit sweater with penny loafers. He is a character in your living room, in the story of your relationship with her. Beyond that, he is somehow your arch rival, the one judge to whom you must prove your worth. You don't realize that her mere acceptance of you is enough to make him happy; you need more than this to be truly secure. Your two nostrils are occupied with the smell of chicken rubbed in fresh herbs roasting in the oven, which your mouth can practically taste already. The hair that has grown into a full beard now on your face reveals the saliva on your chin, as you lick your chops and wonder how much longer until dinner. One hand sits on the armrest, the other on the remote, and one ear is monitoring the rain outside, while the other one is listening for a peep out of the old man to your left.

"Isn't this rain outside amazing?" the old man is muttering now, as he breaks the silence between you.

Suddenly, you can think of nothing more compelling to speak of than the weather. When people, strangers and friends alike, overcome whatever difficulties exist in relating to each other through conversation, they talk about the weather. *Nice day outside today,* they say. *Some heat we've been having,* they say. Neighbor talk, you think. Weather: the subject that exists to bind us all together in this human experience. Weather: the subject that allows you to somehow be human for a moment, to not be a wooly mammoth in her house. What would the world be without the topic of weather, or without any weather to speak of? A total blanket of silence would descend over the whole city almost immediately: horrifying, you think, as it would underline the fact that you've hedged over into the animal kingdom, and might share nothing more than a bark or a growl should anyone approach you in the market or flower store. In fact, you've decided several times before to hug people you've never even met, just because you overhear them talking about the weather. Being approached by a strange gorilla in public is bad enough, but what must they have thought when you interrupted their polite conversations to bear hug your way into their world? Did they realize you just wanted to be loved?

Slowly, you lean back in your chair and raise the volume on the television a single notch. Someone has just scored another touchdown, and the crowds are cheering with glee. The old man is breathing heavily and staring in the direction of the screen again. You can see him out of the corner of your left eye. You wonder what he must be thinking right now, how he must be processing the information conveyed to him in the scene of this room. His very presence confirms his acceptance of animals uniting with humans. Has he fully come to terms with this, or will it suddenly dawn on him in the middle of dessert, as he clutches his steak knife in a fit of rage, attacking that which has threatened the life of his beloved daughter?

You and the old man enter the kitchen as the little girl announces that dinner is served. As if to prove a point, to force the issue or at least to make sure the old man is aware of your relationship together, you approach her and swallow her in an extraordinary hug. Gorilla man and baby girl, hugging before a family dinner in their tiny kitchen, as her father witnesses the display of love, not to be mistaken for anything else. But she is nearly blotted out, your heavy limbs surrounding her the way six feet of dirt might look covering someone accidentally buried alive. You love her, and surely this is no crime, surely the old man can see this. You try to scan for his facial expression out of the corner of your eye, to gauge his reaction to your gesture, to make sure he is not in contempt of this moment. But you can't find him. The long locks of hair have clouded your vision, your eyes shielded now by inches of thick, curly bangs. There is no one to be blamed here, nothing to be said to make the situation any better. Surgery is out of the question for either of you: you will be tall and monster-like and she will be elfin-small forever. Electrolysis is a no-go as well. You learned recently that, priced at forty dollars per half-hour, it would cost you roughly eleven thousand dollars to wipe your body entirely clean of hair, since less than two square inches can be done in one session. You disengage from her and all three of you take your seats at the table.

"Raining like cats and dogs out there," you begin at dinner. Yes, you know you have to bring the conversation back to the weather, and all through the meal, you can tell she is wondering why, not realizing how desperately you are searching for acceptance in the human world. In *their* human world. "Really coming down like reams of paper now," you throw in to the otherwise silent meal, some fifteen minutes after your first attempt. You catch her glaring at you as you mention the rain a second and a third time. You begin to worry a little. Maybe you have gone too far this time, bringing up the weather over and over again, referring to it as "hammers and nails" or "anvils and elephants," anything you can think of to say. Even though you think you've only been discussing the weather in fits and starts, you suddenly realize that you have been rambling on nonsensically for the entire length of dinner, something that you almost never do. "So you see, I don't think that it's really the same because the Tupperware ladies, I believe, used to host the parties in their own homes, and then invite all their friends and their friends' friends over, and then the factory would send out the catalogs and the ladies would all just—" You stop yourself mid-sentence. You don't know the first thing about Tupperware or Tupperware parties, and you can't recall how it was that you stumbled onto the topic in the first place. Last time you remembered, you were suggesting something about the rain, and how it seemed it would never end, and did the old man think it was time to begin constructing an ark together. As dinner grinds to a slow ending, table conversation has dwindled back down to silence. Have you failed her? Can she really accept you, this babbling ape of a thing curiously taking up residence in her human shelter? Doesn't he belong outside in his dog house, instead?

Dinner has ended. The old man left unceremoniously, not entirely rejecting or accepting your attempt at an embrace just before he exited your home. You can't quite wrap your head around the evening, and whether you should judge it as a success or a marked failure to win her over completely. Now, you wash all the dishes in silence. More to the point, you wash the dishes in water, silently. Job detail, kitchen patrol: Hairless: wash duty, gorilla man, dry duty. You sneak a kiss on the back of her neck between drying two of the last glasses. You have offered this as an apology. You have no confidence in your analysis of her mood or the temperature of things between you. This part of the night seems to be going fine when she scampers out of the kitchen, through the bedroom and then into the bathroom. Maybe you spoke too soon. You bolt after her into the bedroom, strip down out of your linen pants, just in case this is your one opportunity, and storm beneath the covers all in one motion like an Olympic hurdler or high jumper. You can hear her washing off her make-up in the bathroom. You've lived together long enough to know all her routines. You gauge her at about the mid-way point now, between the tooth brushing and the astringent, which leaves another seven and a half minutes to go. You lean over to check the time on the clock radio. Nine-thirty. Before you can calculate exactly what time she will be slipping into the bed, given the emotional and psychological exhaustion of your evening, you're out.

All the lights in the house are off. Pitch black, everywhere. The green lights on the bed-side clock display slowly come into focus, as you check to see the time again. The blankets are pulled down to your waist, and you are still quite warm. Hair-shirt. It's a quarter after midnight. How could it have happened? Did she put something in the chicken to make you fall asleep? Was the old man some kind of Jedi Knight, throwing a wicked sleep curse on you before he left so that you wouldn't lay a finger on his daughter? You sound paranoid to yourself, lying there in the dark next to her with these thoughts. You remember the trick you saw on television once, about falling back to sleep at night. You were supposed to remember it for times just like these. First, you put your toes to sleep. Then you put your feet to sleep. Then, your ankles. One by one, your parts are falling back to sleep without you. You hear her purring next to you in quiet, even patterns. Your head is still awake, and you can see the clumps of hair on your belly and your left leg (which is supposed to be asleep), hanging off the bed and out of the covers. Your belly is lit up green-black from the clock light. You are riveted by the hair. There's so much, you think, it's almost like something that doesn't belong to you, a set of in-laws that can't be returned. No one gets this much of anything just for coming into the world one day. You watch it the way you would watch a car crash out in front of your house. You are totally engrossed. You wish that it was 1920 again, and everyone was still wearing fedoras. You think, surely then it would be okay for you to also wear a hat every single day. When you went to sleep at night, you would place it over the clock on the table next to your bed, blocking out the terrifying green light that's shining so brightly on all of that mangy, tangled mess of hair.

AND THEN SOMEHOW, WE FIND EACH OTHER (IN GERMANY, THE CATS)

Seated across from me, separated by not so much as five feet, the slight-ish outline of the woman known as "Zip-Lock" leaned back and forth in her seat, bending at the waist to create the hypnotizing effect of a grandfather clock chime. I don't believe she was humming. Every day, I ride the bus, even when there is nowhere for me to go. I play games with myself like "One Arm Man" and "Molester Mouth." Wearing an oversized coat and tucking one arm behind me, inside my jacket, allowed One Arm Man to register some degree of discomfort on the faces of strangers, as I pretended to keep my balance while standing, asking for help to tie the empty sleeve to the pole that connected the floor to the ceiling. The bizarre rhythms of tongue acrobatics are performed by Molester Mouth while staring directly at a fellow passenger, preferably male, alone and older; these always seemed to make me happy.

Beyond those games, passing time by creating superheroes out of the ordinary denizens of mass public transportation seems like the obvious thing to do. San Francisco buses have a strange way of temporarily making all things equal. When you first enter the bus and sit down, everybody seems the same for a while. Not like they all wear the same uniform as the scene might look were we on our way from prison to the work farm; more like, everyone appears to be of one class or social strata: the bus class. This can easily lull one into a state of reduced awareness. Then one of them pops up unexpectedly, a bona fide superhero in your midst. The last time this happened, I walked right into her, the one called Zip-Lock, or sometimes even referred to as "Flesh Pouch."

Covered from head to toe in loose fitting translucent plastic baggies neatly taped together with clear packing tape, Zip-Lock rocked and swayed, tightly crouched around her white mid-size zippered LeSac hand bag. The sound she emitted was all squishy plastic, a garbage bag filled with an infinite number of plump water balloons and packing bubbles. White shoestring laces drawn into a bow, just beneath her chin hemmed in the elastic piping of the crinkly white plastic hood covering her head and outlining the edges of her face. She was passable as a kind of latter-day Inuit, a space-age Alaskan wanderer of the hermetically sealed tundra, as prepared and advanced in terms of technology as a microwave might have appeared to be in the early '60s suburban kitchen. She wore white dishwashing gloves up to her wrists (where the white plastic haz-mat sleeves were tucked in). She had sea foam blue plastic hospital slippers on over her sneakers. Zip-Lock looked like the older sister of the superhero I called "Tic-Tac." It is possible, however, that this was merely a coincidence.

So transfixed on Zip-lock had I become, that I hadn't yet noticed the woman seated next to me. With three assured taps, she pressed her right index finger into my leg, just above the knee. "She's something else, huh," she said, motioning with a half-nod down to her left hand, which held a clear plastic box filled with white tic-tacs. She forced a few mints out into my palm as the three- and four-level apartment-style dwellings rushed by the windows, like the background panels appearing in so many comic books. "She's quicksand on pause, almost," she added, referring to Zip-Lock and winking in unison with the snapping shut of the plastic box in her left hand. Like she'd been there before.

I had strung together a succession of odd jobs over the last few months, and decidedly quit the last one about a month ago. So when the lady sitting next to me said, "Who are you," I quickly blurted out, "I am a male masseuse, meaning not that I am a man who massages, even though I am, but that I massage men, exclusively. A masseur, if you will. The men are required to shave their backs before they are serviced. I love my job. I do not love men." I flushed, feeling the stain of hot red boil into focus in my cheeks, eyeballing this woman whose own back appeared to slightly arch toward me when I said that. "I mean, I was a male masseuse. I just quit my job a month ago. I really don't love men, though." Exactly whose benefit had I repeated this for, I wondered to myself just then as I fixed my gaze on the back of the balding head in front of me, focusing in specifically on a tiny red mole that resembled a fire ant taking a nap.

She looked down at her toes, exposed in her yellow flip-flops, long enough to get me to stare down at them too. Quietly, she said, "Do you own a couch?"

"My couch is like a soap opera, yes—I own one. It has had many lives: each one vaguely similar to the one before, each owner's memories building up in soft layers across its fabric. Fluids too, I would think—but I suppose that's a bit gross. Maybe a slight over-share. Apologies." She looked past me out the window to my right. The bus made another stop, barely lasting long enough for the two short Chinese tourists to hop down to the sidewalk, requiring a bit of athleticism on their part. I had no idea where we were at this point, somewhere out near the western edges of San Francisco, where buildings resembled more "any city" than the archetypal buildings that crowned the hills of downtown and covered the fronts of so many postcards.

"I can see it close-up now, in my mind," she said. "It's green, with a soft focus on it, like they sometimes do in the soap operas, trying to make everything look so intense that way. There is a faded gold paisley pattern—the shapes match up to look like interlocking peacocks." She paused, her mouth shut tight as it appeared she was working bits of licorice or some other sticky candy free from the spaces in between her teeth. Then slowly, one word at a time, sounding more like clicks than words, "Maybe—I—even owned—it—once." It sounded like an apology for knowing things she wasn't supposed to know. She had described the couch exactly.

I needed to fill up this space between us: urgency. The bus driver called out one of the Avenues, farther out than I had expected, something in the twenties. "Between humans, there is a friction. Materials build up, sweat, dirt, smells... We interact through our shared interest in what we cast off, most of which happens—inadvertently," I said, the way a professor would confide in a favorite student. I couldn't quite gauge her reaction, as this had registered in her face only as a slight curiosity; her eyes grew slightly wider— questioning.

There was this sense of being crowded in, rushed up on, or known all at once with her. Had I said too much? I was only supposed to be out for a ride, on my way to get a haircut. There was something that I had left my house to do, and I was not currently doing it. My shagginess and overgrown mop of a head had perhaps opened me up to this conversation—maybe she had figured me to be one of them, the bus dwellers who do nothing but ride around all day, happy to find shelter somewhere out of the sometimes chilling winds. I realized then that, generally speaking, given the dense sandpaper growth of my beard as well, I could be described by an onlooker as "unkempt."

She blinked a few times, staring down at the floor for a moment, then looked up at me. "I had an idea about your life just now."

"Yeah? What were you thinking?" I supposed she knew I would ask her this.

"I understand you to be a man who is a firm believer in mundane tragedies," she said out of the corner of her mouth, which swelled slightly when she said the word mundane.

"What do you mean by this—I mean—I think I know—but—I want you to tell me." The bus made the first turn in the loop at the western end of its line, rolling down a block full of empty restaurants. It was apparently that space of time between lunch and dinner; I'd been aboard the bus for quite some time, given the fact that it most likely took between ninety minutes and two hours to complete the entire line.

"I mean, something horribly rotten, yet very plain and nearly meaningless: this is the kind of thing you consistently find fascinating." She was beyond matter-of-fact in her delivery, a detective in the interrogation room playing the good cop.

"Please continue," I said, thinking she was on the verge of saying something. I concentrated on her face, which I had begun to notice was altogether cherubic, the healthy puffiness of her pink cheeks outlined by the wispy blonde locks that covered her ears.

"I want to tell you something. I want to tell you that in my mind, we have already met, sometime before now, before just twenty minutes ago." She seemed embarrassed by her own words. My silence indicated to her to continue.

"You were walking down a street," she said with all of the interest of a wise old storyteller addressing the tribe. "There was a menu in the window of a restaurant of dubious ethnicity, and it described nearly every dish a person could possibly imagine. There were Italian chicken Parmesan dishes, Philly cheese-steak sandwiches, pot-stickers and Chinese wok-tossed prawns, salads with catfish and crawdads, oysters in gray fondue, still others. A woman exited this restaurant. A tiny smudge of blue eye-shadow dipped mistakenly into the corner of her eye. This woman, she was me. She smiled at the man, who was suddenly paralyzed."

"That man was I, wasn't he?" I interrupted her, trying desperately to recall if the story she had spun was something that had actually happened, an encounter we may have both shared, a younger version of ourselves engaging with each other. Things like this must surely happen all the time; we're just not ambitious or conscious enough to remember.

She nodded, continuing through the tiny smile that pushed up the corners of her mouth. "Her teeth were askew in such a way that they barely pushed out her lips, a tiny volcano opening out onto the morning air, fleshy hibiscus almost in bloom. The man was transfixed. It seemed he could not help but be drawn in by her mouth, it was the one thing of any importance in all the world. He motioned to her in his mind, as if to say something that couldn't be said, as if he wanted to begin telling her all the things he'd never done before, but only the things that begin with the letter 'm.' Maybe this would make her stay a while. *Massages, manicures, marriage, melancholy,* he mumbled to her back then as she walked down the street away from him, getting smaller in his eyes the farther she wandered. Then—she was gone." She broke off here momentarily.

"What happened then? Is that the end? Why are you telling me this?" The questions poured out, like pellets of grain spilling out of a sack cloth. Even after all this, I noticed Zip-Lock peering over at us, somehow jealous of our engagement, but still teetering on her invisible balance beam, rocking energetically back and forth.

"She turned around suddenly in the story, walked back to him. 'Have you ever made out with a stranger?' she said to him. It was like she'd been reading his mind. She leaned in, kissed him. Her mouth, the swollen flower completely on his, like a pair of tender pink snails the flavor of sweet pickled ginger. Her tongue tasted like sweet mango chutney, roaming the insides of his mouth at that moment."

I closed my eyes when she said mango chutney, maybe just blinking for longer than necessary to savor the moment in the story of an earlier version of me, then hurriedly opened them again, feeling a tinge of embarrassment.

"Her mouth on his made him think of first bites into tiny, ripe apricots. She paused, folded her lips up again, whispered in his ear, 'You smell like warm laundry,' and cooed." She whispered the part about the laundry as well, in a voice that seemed too sexy to have come out of this strange woman.

"I think maybe I am not understanding you." She seemed to be trying to tell me something, perhaps more than I was capable of understanding. I reached my hand over to accept the tic-tacs she had again offered to me, wondering for a moment if they were some kind of strange aphrodisiac, a magical gift from a superhero I most certainly should have recognized. What would she do to me once I was again trapped in her web of storytelling? Maybe she was telling me something I already knew, and I was just failing to recognize the truth.

"He will give her a present one day, the man, a pair of Chinese slippers: turquoise, flat and fraying, and a goldfish, which he knows she will flush down the toilet, an unceremonious burial, as soon as he leaves her." She folded her arms across her chest, tucking each of her small, child-like hands into the unbuttoned sleeves of her shirt, a soft, celery-green blouse depicting a thousand tiny mint leaves only a shade darker than the cloth itself. "I mean we—you and I—we are over before we have even begun," she droned, sadly.

She looked out the window behind my head, as if she had never spoken to me at all. I was agitated, intent on finding myself deeper in the story she had told. "I don't believe you," I insisted, speaking in a tone at once both authoritative and firm. "Here's what really happens in my story: one day she sends him a bouquet of one hundred hibiscus flowers, with the card that shows only a single lipstick kiss, and the words, *From Her.* They spend several years together from that point forward, trying to create the perfect pour of milk, so that just the right amount is in the bowl of cereal each morning: no milk left over without any cereal flakes, and no dampened, soggy cereal left there without enough milk in each spoonful at the end."

Zip-Lock arose now and exited the bus, somehow managing to walk in a straight line while still rocking back and forth. Apparently, it was a thing of permanence attached to her, the same way arms and legs append to anyone else. How long had I been on this bus now, I wondered to myself. "He wakes up one day in the distant future and says to her, 'I'm growing a mustache,' and she will notice the wispy and faint impression of a shadow streaked across his lip. Suddenly, she will know that they are through, that there is nothing else between them. 'It's really a fruitless attempt, isn't it?' she will ask him, staring at the space above his lip, meaning to implicate more than just the hair, meaning to tell him she knows that it is over, perhaps before they have even really started. They will stare at each other without words then, as if to say, 'This space between us, gathering momentum and pushing apart, separate soon, and ending.' They will both be right. There won't be anything else for them to do or say."

During the last several lines, the woman had been nodding resolutely, reminding me of the now-departed Zip-Lock, perhaps taking her cues from her superhero counterpart. "There's one other thing in your story that you have forgotten, a conversation they once had." The bus, long gone out of the western loop now, worming circles around the gristled downtown blocks with the street dwellers beginning their evening crawls out of the building fronts. She looked through me now, through my eyes and out into the street.

"What is it?" I ask, partially knowing the answer to my question.

"She wakes up in the middle of the night. She presses her frozen feet onto the backs of his calves as she often has the habit of doing, and it wakes him up, as it always does. She giggles. 'I think I've figured something out,' he tells her, turning on his side to face her, pressing out words between his half-asleep mouth. 'It's about baggage. Your baggage. It's a condition of non-presence. It means, you are more comfortable living in your past. It means you're never really present with me, in this room, with this green couch and freckled ceiling.' Suddenly awake and startled, she will say to him, 'Is this an exercise for you?' not entirely knowing what she means by this."

"It means, to be frank, that she can never love him until he is in her past," I finish this part of the story for her.

"What are you saying now?" She was slightly thrown, our stories weaving in and out of each other, badly braided words. She popped three tiny mints into her own left palm, stared hard down at them for just a second before she tilted her head back slightly, and tossed them directly down her throat. She coughed a tiny cough, then took another mint in between her finger and thumb, and placed it beneath her tongue.

"Her baggage," I repeated, "it means that until he is living in her past, until he is one of her old problems or memories, to be re-hashed with the next man in her life, he can't really mean anything to her. This thing they share is rendered meaningless; isn't that how my story goes?" I nudged her arm with my left elbow, which slipped off into her ribs, slowly.

"She will change the subject in that version, talk about something she knows he doesn't care about, something he will feign the utmost interest in. 'You know the cats in Germany, they don't move the same way the cats do in San Francisco, the way they move in the States, that is,' she will tell him. 'In San Francisco, they're skittish. They bolt at the slightest whisper. But you can just walk right up to them in Germany, and they don't move at all. Just walk right up to one of the cats on the sidewalk, pick it up in your hand, and drown it in a river, if you want to.' 'If you want to,' he will repeat softly to her." She stared down at her feet again, and so did I. Yellow flip flops, ten tiny toes all in a line like a row of pink molars spread across a dentist's operating tray.

Minutes went by. Zip-Lock had been gone for some time. There was the distinct possibility that we had run the entire loop upwards of three times. Leaning into me, she said, "If you could be anywhere in the world right now, where would you be?" Sadly, she said this. It was as if she knew what came next.

Shifting my weight back toward her, I told her all in one breath, "I would be in Paris watching the end of Shark Week on the Discovery Channel France one sweltering August in a small apartment somewhere in the Eleventh Arrondissement." I paused, thinking it the right thing to do just then, possibly for nothing more than dramatic effect. "Do you know why?" I asked her, knowing then by the look in her face, the sly smile that had suddenly appeared, she most certainly knew the answer.

Seconds passed.

I started in again, saying, "Because when all the programming is coming to an end, and it's almost the end of the week of twenty-four-hour shark information shows, the French television station, unlike Shark Week broadcast on any other station anywhere else in the world, closes out the final day with—"

She interrupted me here, finishing my thought, the way she'd been trained to do, the way she did every time she found herself in a moment exactly like that one, "With a slate gray title card that reveals the word in three black, capitalized letters: 'FIN.'"

MY FRIEND THE PORNOGRAPHER

"I really like it when they look super young," Toots says. We're heading south. I'm sitting in the passenger seat of his old Volvo. It's sky blue.

After a pause, "What's such a turn-on about that? I mean—" it was hardly a question, really.

"I don't know. Their skin is like, rubbery or something. You can press on their butts, and it like, springs back up from underneath. Sooo sexy." He says that like he is excited about telling me the recipe for his favorite meal or something. Toots looks convinced, leaning on his seat, arms stacked and folded over the top of the steering wheel.

"Do you make them wear pajamas or pigtails or anything?" This hangs there, nearly disregarded. He merges over a lane to the right, eyeing the rear-view mirror from the very top corner of his vision. Did I say that loud enough? He's twenty-five. That's not even his real name, but I think he admitted to me that it sounds good to him, and what's the difference, really, when it comes down to it? His real name is Will.

"It has more to do with what's real. It can't be faked." He seems upset, sits back and corrects his posture, straightening. He's been doing seventy this whole time. "It's real. Their skin. They giggle and stuff. It's weird. It's not about a costume or anything. It's weird." Dwelling on that, Toots looks over his left shoulder. Maybe he's thinking about turning.

"Do they let you kiss 'em?" That's a serious question. We both know how important that is. Tonight, we're shooting a scene for "Darkmeat.com." It'll be my first. This is mostly what Will does on Monday nights. We go under a bridge.

"When they do, it's amazing. It makes it more real, which is the goal. I try to make that happen every time, I mean, it's awkward. My fans or whatever – they look for that. It makes it a major turn-on, which is weird. It's my favorite part, when they get nervous, which is just like real life. Sometimes I tell myself I won't do it anymore. Then it just comes up. I love it when they look so young."

Toots strings together his thoughts like this all the time. Dense and fragmented, one has to pay close attention. There is no space between words, which I think he does on purpose. It's like he's just thinking the stuff all the time, and then he opens his mouth, and some stuff in there trails out into the room or whatever. He's only twenty-five. Somehow he knew the industry was only ever a phone call away.

"I think I like it when they look really young too." This thing we have in common. "Only they're like, eighteen though, right? I mean, for real?" That sounds too professional. I've never been on a real set before, and maybe

I'm nervous or something. Will is smoking a cigarette now. It's natural.

When we finally get to Long Beach, things seem pretty normal. It's like seven or something, nearly dark, and now I'm not that nervous. I'm holding a stage light and a camera bag. The bag's zipper is broken somewhere at the corner, so the whole thing just sort of sags open like a big leather mouth. We're walking to another car to meet someone. All the streetlights in Long Beach got replaced with these orange bulbs at some point, or maybe they're more like amber. It's tough not to feel like something amphibian when you're in this city. It's like everything is under close inspection. I'm looking at Herb, I think. He's got a light in his hand, too.

Toots and Herb exchange hugs near the back of Herb's black sport utility, which is overly clean. "Are you ready for tonight man?" Toots asks. He's already told me enough about Herb for me to know the answer to the question. I guess all Herb really does is fuck and maybe talk online some.

"Is this girl gonna be here on time tonight, 'cause if she don't get here by like, nine or something, I got two other girls on the hook for later." He's more calm than either of us. This is pretty much his normal thing, and I think he's mostly over it. "Hey, man," he says, looking at me. He puts his hand out. Now I'm shaking it, trying hard not to look nervous. He closes the back gate and window, which makes the silver rope chain around his neck bounce slightly off his chest.

Herb knows the code for the apartment building, which we're walking towards. When he dials us in, the door buzzes for a second and then clicks, almost like a jail. We walk inside. Luther lives on the second floor, or maybe the third. The lights in the apartment building are amber. It's one of those buildings where there's all this outdoor shared space: open hallways leading to everyone's doors, utility carpeting covering everything but the concrete stairs and the deck around the pool. Stairs going everywhere surround the pool in the middle of the courtyard, which is too big for the space. There must be more than a hundred units in the complex. Herb leads the three of us to Luther's door and takes out his key. I wonder if this is his apartment for a second. Maybe that's because now I'm nervous, though. Herb and Luther share everything, Toots says. He told me double penetration is their favorite.

The thing they're doing is highly organized as far as any social situation goes, meaning they all have a part in it that is defined and well-structured. It's like a programmed mission, which allows them to all get comfortable. That makes the part before she gets there weird. Like now is when we all have to be real, or something. Only Luther's apartment smells like salty crotch-sweat. I wonder if it smells like that all the time, or if it's just his feet. I would have to skip showering for like three days to cultivate that kind of ripeness. Besides that though, Luther is a neat freak. The blinds are drawn and maybe the window's closed, because of the smell, which is trapped, organic and dense. Luther's back in the bedroom on the phone before he comes out and shakes everyone's hand.

"I never said that anyways. Look, I think I had too much to drink. I was at a barbecue today and I drank too much. Yes, I am still there. I don't think it would be too wise for me to drive down to you right now, baby. No, I never said that." Luther is obviously giving some girl the run-around for whatever reason, and he holds the "shhh" finger up to his mouth as he offers each of us something to drink. He's wearing boxers, a white t-shirt and dark sunglasses. It's difficult to see anything. I think he's like six-four, or maybe an inch shorter than Herb. When he asks me, in sign language, if I want a drink, I say "no" back to him with similar hand signs. Herb pulls out his laptop. He's setting it up on one of the emptier desks.

A few seconds later, Luther goes back into the bedroom and I walk into the kitchen to the refrigerator for a beer. I'm not sure why I did that, only maybe I am nervous or something. I can't tell right now. I smell vinegar when I open the refrigerator, which makes me realize the smell from a few minutes ago has kind of subsided, or else I just got used to it. There's raw turkey or ground chicken or something on one shelf, and a six pack of Heineken on another. I take a bottle. The bottle opener is a magnet on the refrigerator door, but it's difficult to make it work the right way. I sit back down in the room next to Herb. Luther's off the phone now. He's pouring sugar out of a bag into a pitcher, making Kool-Aid. I'm looking around the apartment. It kind of looks like a cheap office. Maybe it's because I'm nervous. It's after eight now.

"Bitches, let me tell you, man," he says, stirring the pitcher with a wooden spoon and pretty much just talking, not really to anyone, "they just want from you. You give 'em the dick, and then they expect all this shit. And I was just fuckin' her at like, 40 percent of my shit, and she was complainin' about how she was hurt and everything." None of us knows exactly what to say about this, and Luther's letting it hang there out in the space with us for a second. Herb's checking his email, excited about some pictures a woman sent to him of her, standing nude and leaning over the kitchen counter. Will went into the bedroom a minute ago to take a piss or something. Maybe Luther's cultivating his persona, I'm not sure, because he *is* on the set I guess, and then he says, "Imagine if I was bangin' her at like 90 percent or whatever. I'd have to use some of my nursing shit on her afterwards." I think Will said Luther was like an x-ray technician or something on the side, so that's kind of like being a nurse. I think he also told me he spent some time in the armed forces. I'm guessing Marines. There's a black sticker on the refrigerator, that I just noticed, that says "orgasm donor" in white letters. I'm looking at the diagrams in a book called *Teach Yourself Black Belt Karate* that I found on the kitchen counter, written by some famous guy. It all seems so complicated.

There isn't really a couch, and Herb's pulling out a pair of mattresses that are covered in plastic and leaning on a wall near the window. He's still wearing a baseball cap, which is black with no letters or pictures. Will comes out of the bathroom. He was in there way too long, I think. "You know there's like an eight-foot python on the floor in there?" he's asking mostly me. "I think I got trapped in there for a minute."

There are five desks around the perimeter of the room, and computers on all of them. It's obvious they've done this before. "That's my daughter, Baby. And that's her room in there, so pretty much nobody can ask her to move. She's my roommate." Luther's way too matter-of-fact not to actually mean that. Herb lays out the mattresses in the middle of the floor, and Luther throws a clean sheet on top of them. Or maybe it isn't, I'm not sure, because I decide not to touch it. My first instinct is to get up and help Herb make the bed, only I'm still sitting, shuffling through the karate book again, looking at diagrams of flipping techniques. Herb sets up a few lights, which are too bright and pointed up at the ceiling, so he only turns them on and off again, and I get up to set up the light I brought in from Will's car.

There is a framed picture of ex-Dodgers pitcher Fernando Valenzuela on the bookcase and a few stacks of old Elvis movies on the top shelf, which is lined mostly with lesser-known pop-mystery novels by Dean Koontz and Steven King. I make a couple of circles around the room and turn on the fan in the corner when Luther notices me fingering the spines of the books. "No one borrows my books, man. No one. Please don't even take any of them off the shelf." I can tell he's serious. That exchange was normal, so it felt real, which makes me calm. We are still waiting for the girl to show up. I guess they flake a lot, from what Toots says. He's talking with Herb. Luther's signing a release form, which I glance at quickly on my way to get another beer, and notice he's twenty-four. Herb's says he's forty-one.

"You need to let us take a few Polaroids of 'em. Look at it this way; we show up on time, and they're always late. We perform at an outstanding level, on time, every time. How many nuts do we give you every time? Five? Luther? Six?" Herb looks in Luther's direction when he says that. Luther's wearing a blue kerchief on his head, which is holding back his short dreadlocks, and still has his sunglasses on. They're completely black. "Sometimes they don't even show up. And if I'm gonna be late cuza traffic or whatever, I always call. Right? *Always.* Don't I deserve something extra for that?" It comes out of him like a long ribbon of words, curling and connected, without much breath in between. He's sounding almost like Will, only Herb has a bit of a lisp. I think that's his real name, too.

Will is seriously considering this, but I think it's got him a little bit upset, too. "You can't post them on your site," he says, maybe only because Herb's had his laptop out of his duffel bag and wired in to one of Luther's online connections this whole time. The wire he uses to tie in is like a hundred feet long and green. Herb had to walk into the other room with it just to make the connection, spreading the cable out along the floor. "You guys are getting way too ahead of yourselves. These chicks are hot, and you get paid. You fuck 'em bareback, as much as you want. That's because of me. Let's not forget any of that." I think that's more Toots than Will, because it is so business-like. Herb backs down a bit now. It's getting closer to nine, which is the time we decided would be the last call before wrap-up, if she wasn't going to show. Now we're just four guys in a room.

When Candy Pink gets here, I go back downstairs and let her in, which is exciting and weird, but the fresh air is nice, too. The pool lights are on now, which I think is somehow romantic. One of her eyes is a little too close to the middle, like a little cross-eyed, but it's really kind of endearing in a cute way, and not at all ugly. She has a funny nose and she's a bit pigeon-toed in her bouncy walk. She's wearing tight black daisy-dukes, a hot pink string bikini top underneath a black zip-up windbreaker, and tennis shoes, which are white. All in all, I think she's sexy, but more like a little slutty, though I'm not sure if that's just the context we're both in. I try to imagine how I would think of her if this was a health club we were in, but I can't get the thought to crystallize completely, and it's hard to make that call. Right now, it's all pretty much out there in the open.

I follow her up the stairs. I don't pay enough attention to tell whether it's two or three flights up. It's confusing. Looking at her from behind, I get the impression she's got the type of body that looks just okay in clothes, but then naked, she's probably like worth a lot of drool. I'm actually thinking about this when she looks back at me, and I have to quickly look up from staring at her ass to tell her it's gonna' be the first door there on her right. I'm more embarrassed now than nervous.

When she walks into the room, I'm still behind her, and now Herb and Luther seem on edge, or at least impressed and remotely turned on. Nearly thirty seconds go by with no one really moving much. Candy is sort of on display. It's tough to tell with the sunglasses on, but Luther's hardly paying any attention to her at all now, sipping his Kool-Aid, so I can tell he kinda' likes her. Herb mumbles, "Oh good, yes, good," to himself as he tests the lights again or something. He's fidgeting. I'm following her into the back bedroom, but she pauses for a second to show everyone who she is again. Will's ready to start working, but he *is* checking her out. He looks at me and sort of raises his brow in some sign of being pleased or whatever. I think Candy Pink is the only one who's not really nervous. She's just at work, so I pick up the camera before I go back into the bedroom with her.

Candy has two luggage-sized bags with her: one's pink, and the larger one is white. I carried them up the stairs. I guess part of the deal is that she shows up and then has to put her makeup on or whatever, before anything can happen. Maybe that makes it more like Hollywood than porn somehow, which is fine with me, because I just want to talk with her a bit and get some "behind the scenes" kind of footage. Her cell phone rings. It's her babysitter, who I guess tells her everything is alright back at home. She's got a little girl; I just know it. Will has urged me to try to get some real stuff on tape. I think this is what he means, so I go hand-held, and shoot both her and her reflection in the mirror at the same time. She hangs up the phone. The lighting in the bedroom is more like a smoky lounge than anything. Candy's putting on her makeup. Her pink bag was filled with it.

I'm asking her stupid questions like how long has she been doing porn, and does she like it, and are there things she either won't do in porn that she will only do with her real lovers, or the opposite, while she finishes putting on her makeup. She takes off her windbreaker and asks me to help her decide what to wear. We've sort of become friends already I guess. "Do you like the pink? Okay. Wait. Hold on. Or the white one?" She pulls out two very small pieces of fabric that look more like swatches for interior designers than actual clothes.

"Go with the pink. It's more about what you are, right? I mean, that's your thing." She giggles a nervous laugh. She does that almost every time she says anything. Sometimes, that's all that comes out.

I make sure to ask if it's okay that I watch her changing, which seems weird right after I say it, but it's more interesting maybe than what's about to happen in the other room, so it appears to be natural. I think she gets that, and lets me stay. "What about the shoes? Are you going to wear heels?" That's my thing, so I guess I have to ask. She's pulling them out of her other bag as I'm asking, and she smiles at me when she puts them on. They're way too high to be comfortable. We walk into the room together, slowly.

"I kinda' have to go to the bathroom," Candy giggles to everyone and no one. She's standing right up next to me now, so I feel like I have to be the one to help her, only I'm easily more afraid of snakes than she is. I notice a bit of foundation powder has rubbed into the skin right above one of her eyebrows, and I lean into her face, rubbing the spot with the edge of my thumb. She doesn't ask why or say anything. I don't know how much of her personal space she feels like she actually owns, especially in this moment.

"Hey Candy, can you get out your driver's license and stuff? I wanna' get you swearing on camera and everything." Will is Toots again, 'cause this is the business part. All the girls have to swear on camera before anything happens that they are there of their own free will, about to engage in an act of sexuality that they are completely freely choosing. She swears, and I get a close-up of her driver's license, which says her real name and her age, which is thirty. "Hey can I smoke before I pee and before we shoot? Does anybody smoke?" Candy is looking around again. All the action seems to move around her.

We're sitting on the concrete steps, talking quietly and smoking. Candy smokes extra-long cigarettes. "Are you nervous?" That's all I want to know. I think she knows I'm serious, and interested.

"No. Well, kind of, but not really," she says sweetly. This feels like a real conversation any two people might have, and she finishes, "Are you?" I giggle at the question, so she knows I am, and she starts to giggle too.

"Let's go," I say more friendly than professionally, and I offer to stamp out her cigarette for her since she's barefoot.

Fucking on camera reeks of insincerity, which is a fact. I help Candy into the bathroom, and even sit in there while she pees, and then we come out into the room and that's when it starts. Luther and Herb seem to know what they're doing, jockeying around Candy like it's more about play-wrestling than sex. I think they're all just trying to get their bearings or something. I'm more paying attention to the little circular indentations the concrete steps left in Candy's ass from our conversation outside. Toots is craning around the mattresses, catching the action in the popped-out screen on the side of the camera, not really watching what's in front of him at all. I wonder if anyone is actually enjoying this.

Luther's cock is in Candy's mouth. That's how all this starts; like in one second she's on the bed with the sound of crinkling plastic, her shoes are back off and Herb is pulling her breasts out of her dress, which comes off shortly after that. He crawls under her and laps at her pussy while

Luther's still got his sunglasses on, I guess staring at his own dick going in and out of her mouth. The whole thing's like so far removed from anything tactile or real, it's like it may as well not even be happening. When Toots makes a pass around the room with the camera, I have to circle around behind him so I don't get caught on tape. It's all part of the deal.

They take turns fucking her for what seems like forever. They run through the typical battery of positions, then decide to take a short break. The room smells ripe again, a little like rotting potatoes and warm citrus fruit, maybe. The whole thing's been vaguely uninspiring, and I really want to talk about it with her. Now we're back outside, on the steps. Maybe it's desperation. We don't say much this time, and I force myself to ask about what just happened.

"Are you into this at all, 'cause..." I prompted her to say whatever she really wanted to. I wish I had the camera with me. But maybe that would have ruined it.

"I don't know—I guess. Their rhythm sucks. It's all off or something. I mean, it's okay." That's the first time she doesn't giggle. She takes a drag, which seems too long, like she's trying to bury a breath underneath all that smoke, way down deep inside her. She looks at me, smiling.

"Their cocks aren't that big. I was unimpressed." I don't know how much she's willing to analyze the situation, but that doesn't mean I don't want to talk about it. It is porn, after all, and once you're right in the middle of it, you realize just how many givens you've taken for granted in a moment like what just happened.

"That's usually better, trust me. If it's too big, it just hurts, believe me, you can't pay me enough. That's not even fun." This is sincere. I mean, she really means that. It's her talking.

"They seem like, a little high school-ish, or something. Like, overly enthusiastic, maybe. Like they aren't really paying that much attention to what's going on." I'm more wondering to myself than asking her directly. "Are you gonna' kiss them?"

She waits a second before she answers. "No."

We walk back up the stairs for Round 2.

When I walk her to her car later, after it's all over, we are alone, and I ask Candy for her phone number. I don't know what that means about me, but I know I have to do it. I started thinking about it when I was watching her shower, after all the sex. I had to protect her from the snake, which was asleep with its tongue in its mouth on the shelf just below the green towels. That part felt normal to me, even though she said no when I asked her if I could wash her hair. Candy thought I was joking, but I'm pretty sure I was serious about that. She says "Sure," meaning yes, about her phone number, which comes out before that childish nervous laugh, and adds, "I'll write it on a big piece of paper, so you won't lose it."

Her pen writes in pink. It adds to her thing, I think. I'm not nervous anymore, because this is almost like real life again, and I'm okay with that. She's sitting up high in her truck, which seems so huge for her, even though she's close to perfect body-wise, and not really petite. I wonder for a second if the beach chair she put in the truck bed will fly out on the freeway drive back home to the Valley. I guess she doesn't care. I really want to hug her, even more than I want to have sex with her, which I don't even think I want at all. She has the sexiest back I think I've ever seen, which is a strange thing to think about a person, especially when it's true.

"So get out of the truck and give me a hug already," I say firmly to her, but with sincerity, or at least it sounds that way to me. I can't wait to hug her now. She hops out and *holds* me more than she *hugs* me, and maybe a little too long, at that, but it's nice, and I think it's been the only real thing that's happened to her tonight. She bounces a little onto her tippy-toes, which I can see now because I am looking down over her shoulder at the ground behind her. I let go.

"Call me, 'k?" It comes out more cutesy than maybe she intends it to, but I think she might actually mean it. It's so easy to get deluded in a situation like this. I don't know if I'm even gonna call her now, or ever, for that matter. But maybe we could just have ice cream together, pistachio, which is my favorite, and then just hug, and that could probably be great. She drives away, and I stand there for an extra second before going back inside, trying to process the entire night. I realize I'm thinking about her daughter now, and wondering if she's asleep yet, and maybe what she's dreaming about.

OHNE TITEL (DER PUNKT)

The color of the spot on my foot is such that it cannot be described in relative terms, which is to say, the spot is a "black coffee brown" as compared to the more "ruddy pink" flesh that surrounds it.

This would fail to explain why I can then see it clean through my shoe, why I see it constantly in dreams, why within minutes of meeting any woman, the spot is there, plainly reflected in her face, calling my name, naming me. No, the color of the spot on my foot cannot be described in terms of the visual; instead, it is best understood by proxy, through another sensate experience; it is *the taste of blood in my mouth*: foreign and independent, though at once inherently connected.

The spot on my foot is more than just a spot. It's an obstruction, a giant tree, standing perfectly and absurdly straight, growing upright from the middle of the deep end of the pool in the backyard of every house I ever grew up in. No one climbs this tree, no one in the neighborhood asks after its origins. Children visiting the house to play during my grammar school years pretended not to see it, indeed, heaved themselves off the diving board directly at it. At the last moment, shifting directions, adjusting airspeed, flapping their soggy arms as if intending to fly over it, only to end up planted somewhere near the meeting point of the majestic trunk and the placid surface of the lukewarm water.

But I knew they noticed. They pissed themselves, underwater, pissed on the base of the tree, the spot on my foot, in that pool. And in their hidden disgust, marking their territory, I was somehow alternately repulsed, guilty, and immensely proud. I *was* the spot on my foot.

Point One: Distraction and History
(To Get So Close That You Cannot See)

As I grew older, I invented methods to draw attention near it, but not directly at it, thinking that this might somehow allow me to maintain a degree of quiet honesty with others and myself. Further, I reflected on a truth that I had seen in action countless times: after all, what was less obvious to a person than the quotidian, the banal, the refuse of every ordinary life consisting of nameless piles of disregarded stuff, always right there in our sight, but never fully acknowledged?

There were various historical models that I pursued and examined during the development of this hypothesis. I was seventeen, smoked cigarettes without inhaling, jangled coins in my pockets to an imaginary rhythm, wrote letters to editors of newspapers overseas, which I clumsily translated by way of pocket dictionaries, first from English to Portuguese, then from Portuguese to French. I ate plum flavored jam on toast with cheese. All of the historical models I studied had ended up in horrible and overwhelming defeat, but that did nothing to deter me.

In the spring of 1945 the Russian army assumed four positions in their tactical surrounding of Berlin. Germany, now at the end of her second attempt to take over the world, was near to falling.

Hitler had ordered the people of the city to protect the surrounding suburbs with every bit of their very flesh and marrow, thinking that the wall of impenetrable humans would somehow dissuade the Russians from marching.

Ordinary citizens, play-acting the parts of soldiers, fortified their positions at the edges of Berlin as the Red Army pounded the buildings for eight days straight, slowly encroaching, meter after meter, effectively strangling the city from the outside in. The outer suburbs were quickly laid to rubble; the strategy failed miserably, the residents of the city suffered horrendously and lost everything—food, home, will.

Though they had stood in unison as a human shield, a testament to the unified will of the central city, they had served instead as targets for the enemy, standing there, absorbing every mortar aimed in their direction.

In Berlin, the inner rings of the city fell shortly after. For me, this was *history worth paying attention to.* After a close study of this model, I concluded that I would wear brashly colored striped socks every day, in a concentrated effort to attract the unsuspecting gaze of every onlooker.

They could be lead to the exact area where they could destroy me; lead by the hand to the shelf and cabinet wherein my Achilles heel was kept, all in the hopes of ultimately misleading them through subtle and sly trickery: the citizen soldiers there to protect my beloved capital city.

The socks! Impossible blood reds alternated with an olive green the color of prehistoric foliage, which together vibrated intensely, both attracting and temporarily blinding anyone looking down near my feet. *Look near the spot, you!* I was a fool, a clown.

Point Two: Disdain and Psychology (The Matter of the Corporate Bureaucracy)

I began to hate people, no, humanity in general, and had few friends, or rather, several acquaintances in the corporate bureaucracy who, out of sympathy, regularly invited me out to different social events. I looked into their eyes during such uncomfortable moments, suffering through the humiliation of their invitations, feigning a pitiful glee, all the while knowing they merely wanted fodder for jokes and stories at next year's annual Christmas party.

Whatever they could think of to get my shoes off in public, they tried. We went roller-skating at least once a month. After several years of this, my coworkers were Olympic-caliber athletes; they shared speed records and argued over petitioning the committee for an exhibition sport consideration in the games of 2020. They gnawed constantly on scraps of handheld food like anxious, craven rabbits, destroying fistfuls of tuberous vegetables with riotous verdant plumes at their tops, their breath smelling like hot carrots and celery; they were wretched.

Watching them all from the rafters where I would climb after sneaking away and changing back out of my skates, the members of the bureaucracy would become tiny NASCAR competitors, endlessly bucking and straining around the ellipsis of the rink, frantically trying to outpace the others.

Ice-skating, hot tub parties, car washing fundraisers —their ploys were shameless. But knowing my part in the grand scheme of their lives and this story, I humbly acquiesced.

At work, I developed crushes on all of the women in lower administrative positions; I perceived this to be the only way to exact my revenge on the bureaucrats: in secret, I loved their helpers. Never before had I bestowed so much genuine and unrequited love on such a banal litany of questions: *Can I borrow your stapler? How are you liking the smaller post-it notes this season? Did you get the black or the pinto beans during the Springtacular Company Event…?*

The simple irony in the existence of the spot nowhere less than on my foot does not escape me: but an "unsuitable substitute" for what exactly, I think. I ponder the meaning of Freud's language, "an executive weakness of the sexual apparatus," and immediately and uncontrollably turn to thoughts of the fifth-level female administrators, with their cropped or otherwise equally restrained hair, who serve the lowest echelon in the first order of the corporate bureaucracy.

I keep them close to my thoughts, harbor these vigilantly, as the dock and tugboats cradle the mammoth shipping vessels and containers that line the ports. Thusly, I will not let the spot on my foot become detached from the particularity of myself, the individual.

Together, we are one.

Point Three: Discovery and Ethnography (Bathing and Loathing)

I spoke no German in Cologne when I first visited during a vacation from the corporate headquarters in my mid-twenties. Every morning, I ventured out from my hotel chamber and down the street to the tobacconist, where I bought the English papers.

Reading the news over coffee and toast in the intimate confines of the café, I drew pictures every morning of my eggs, offering these instead of a verbal order to the waitresses, who only smiled uncomfortably, returning sometime later with a plate of toast covered with eggs, by order of my drawing.

My spot traveled overseas, I saw it in their faces, I saw it clearly described in the tiny yolk of the fried egg drawing on the blank white sheet of paper I turned over to them, every morning, when I knew they knew.

How could I then love them? Those German girls, with their particular aversion to striped socks.... I did everything possible to solidify my relationship with them, cradled my cigarette more gently, ate with fork and knife all at once, smiled only with the corner of my mouth like a mad jackal in heat.

I sat there at breakfast and imagined the waitresses, each of them singularly, stumbling upon my hotel room as I entered or exited, the fantasy alternating between the two, whereupon they requested permission to use my bath, or some other such activity involving my bathroom to prepare or clean themselves. There, I would study them, an ethnographer and a pervert, quietly taking sturdy mental notes. Eventually, after a time devoted entirely to preening, they would invite me into the bath.

For what seemed like hours in the fantasy, I would be sitting on the closed toilet seat, admiring their level of self-absorption and their simultaneous ability to ignore me, startled at the resistance of their skin to pruning after so much time submerged, all the while thinking solely of the spot on my foot. They could love me, surely, but then—how could they love that spot?

To bathe was to reveal, to reveal was to surrender, to surrender was to suffer the complications of mockery and to therefore be doomed to exile and loneliness. I returned home shortly thereafter, to Corporate Headquarters, and continued to borrow the stapler.

Point Four: Shopping

The opposite of play is not what is serious, but what is real. These are the words printed on my favorite t-shirt, which I have made seven versions of, each a different shade of pink, each with the abbreviated name of a corresponding day of the week on the back.

At the mall where I had the iron-on letters placed on the shirts (all in black capitals of a soft felt) the girls behind the counter could not have been more than sixteen years old. They smoothed out the t-shirts on the counter in front of me, their taut, flexed digits ending in manicured nails too long to be taken seriously, with white-striped cartoons of themselves leaving temporary scratched lines where they confirmed the location of the lettering on each of the pink shirts. The finger, an exposed terminus of the body, like my foot and the spot would have been in that German bath. Through those fingers, could the mall girls not identify with my secret? Could they not see the spot on the other side of the counter, below them, hovering there, shielded by the striped socks and my unconvincing smile?

Now I wear the shirts underneath my white collared shirt and tie, sport coat, and on colder winter days, my great navy wool overcoat. There, the phrase hides, an attachment and extension of me, echoing the spot on my foot, the locus of my isolation, my self-imposed exile. I move out from my apartment into the street all in one motion. *To play is to remain always in one place, which confirms then that movement is a necessary version of the real.*

A Truncated Compendium of Statistics Concerning

Four states lead the nation in cycling deaths: California, Florida, New York, and Texas, which accounted for 43 percent of all bicycle deaths in the year 2003. Auto crashes represent the leading cause of death for bicycling people aged 6-27, males aged 6-23 and 26. The first automobile crash in the United States occurred in New York City in 1896, when a motor vehicle collided with a bicyclist, severing both legs below the knee and effectively bleeding out the victim, who could not be saved by doctors, and died in the dusty street, staring down at the limbs, now foreign, though only moments before, attached.

Of the many bicycling accidents in the state of California, more than 67 percent occur within the vicinity of, or adjacent to, sites where other sporting events are either taking place, have taken place in the past, or will take place in the future.

The second historical appearance of a two-wheeled riding machine was in 1865, when instead of pushing one's feet against the ground, pedals were applied directly to the front wheel. This machine was known as the velocipede, or "fast foot." It was popularly known as the Big Cat Bone Shaker, since it was also made entirely of Manzanita wood, having a beautiful leopard design, where small spots of deep burgundy bark naturally flaked away to reveal a lovely olive shade beneath.

Point Five: Defeat
(Bicycles, Tanks and a Change of Pace)

And so it was a Wednesday night, around half past eight. I, in my late twenties now, invited out once again by the members of the corporate bureaucracy, this time to a bowling night function at some local lanes. Knowing full well that the event offered another installment of their supposedly covert strategy, wherein I would by necessity have to change into proper sporting footwear squarely in front of them, thereby exposing the stripes and the spot, I went anyway, once again playing my part.

It was a brisk evening, too cold for early spring, and I fancied myself somehow not unlike the soldiers of the Red Army, heading anxiously onward to Berlin, prepared for war and knowing full well the situation that lay ahead, the corporate bureaucracy's version of Adolf Hitler Platz, *der bowling alley*. Surely it's no accident that the Germans have over fifteen words that roughly translate in English to *spot*, including platz, punkt and pickel. Surrounded by myself, I was to be defeated by my spot, my punkt, my pickel.

Traveling west on Main Boulevard in the lane closest to the sidewalk, I slowed down a block or two after Pass Avenue; I was looking for the bowling alley: the MarLanes. From a short distance, I saw the sign for the cross-street I had been searching for, and slowed down considerably, as I knew the bowling alley was close. I discarded a cigarette out the driver's side window, letting my hand hang aimlessly outside for an extra second. The radio was off, though I could somehow hear the news inside my head.

When I saw the entrance to the parking lot, it appeared at once vaguely familiar, as I had been there before on trips with the corporate bureaucracy, though for some reason, it came upon me suddenly. I was not traveling terribly fast, maybe ten miles an hour, as I had slowed down even more after noticing the cross-street up ahead only moments before. I made a hard right into the parking lot of the bowling alley and heard a sudden and distinct scratching sound towards the rear passenger side of the vehicle. In a flash, I felt several eyes upon me, faces appearing from out of nowhere lining the parking lot, seemingly curious and hostile.

The sound, insistent and unique, might best be described as the sound a large tree branch might make when scratching against a slab of metal, not unlike the tanks of the red army, poised before battle in the forests at the outskirts of Berlin. When they took to their offensive, how their temporary disguise within massive shrouds of tree branches must have sounded, clawing their way off the iron and falling dumbly to the forest floor, arboreal traitors and their graves.

This had all happened too suddenly for me to be scared; indeed, fear was not an option. Only a few short years earlier, I had been drawing pictures of my breakfast in a foreign land to beautiful girls who I had envisioned bathing in my dirty tub, and now this. But what was *this*? For the first time in my life, things had happened with such immediacy, with such complete urgency, that I can recall now those precious few minutes when I did not think of the spot on my foot.

The car lurched as I engaged the foot brake and set it in the park position. I frantically exited the vehicle to see what had happened, imagining the obscene and pondering the further harsh cruelties that might be visited upon me in this world.

I had parked in the sidewalk, halfway out into the street and halfway into the parking lot. I ran around the side of the vehicle, as instinctively I believed the noise had come from over my right shoulder, near the rear of the car. The red tail-lights cast a strange glare, a low-level emergency warning that I was foolish not to notice at the time.

Beneath the yellowish circle of the streetlights and behind the car, near the curb, was a young man. He, perversely tangled up in the frame of his bicycle, looked like a landed version of an octopus in a fisherman's still damp net. Somehow he had too many limbs, and for some reason, the bicycle appeared limp, strategically draped around the boy's body like a spider's web around a fly.

And so it dawned on me that here was the blunt explanation for the noise I had previously heard. It was not immediately that I came to realize I was the perpetrator of such violence, that I had somehow caused this scene, much to the delight of the onlookers in the parking lot on that chilly Wednesday night. So this is what they mean when they refer to an *accident*, I thought to myself, feeling a dull sense of removal from the moment.

I theorized: If I had no idea what happened at all, even to the point of feeling almost entirely uninvolved, then can it still be called an accident? And further, how does it feel to be a confirmed misanthrope, to have come this close to inadvertently eliminating one of *them*, and yet—to have failed, without realizing that one was even making an attempt? *Could one's subconscious be put on trial?*

At this point, several facts became clear to me all at once. 1) The rider was a male, young, wearing what appeared to be semi-professional riding gear, all of which was black. 2) The bike itself was black, although there was a headlight mounted on the handlebars; the light was switched on. 3) I had never seen the bike in my rearview, and judging from this, I assumed he had been riding very close to the side of the vehicle, and perhaps even in my blind spot, for a distance of several hundred feet, only as slowly or quickly as a bicycle might travel. 4) The rider was not wearing a helmet.

I bent down, and knelt there for some time next to the man, who appeared to be in his late teens or early twenties. His face was smooth, and as he winced, freckles on his cheeks doubled over on each other in the folds of skin nearest his eyes. What at first appeared to be a gently resting ladybug just behind his ear turned out to be a life-sized tattoo of the same insect, in a rich grass-like green, hovering gracefully on his neck.

I asked him if he was okay, and he moved himself around slightly, angling his neck and back, and then propping his head on a sweatshirt handed to him by a witness in the area, a stout mustachioed man walking down the street at the time, with a half-eaten candy bar and small, dirty hands.

I asked him if I could do anything for him, maybe get him water, to which he replied that he had a backpack on with water in it. I noticed the water-spout and tube which hung over his right shoulder, dangling there on his arm. I asked him if he was cold, or hurt, while others were asking after his health, pain, etc. He said that he felt a bit dizzy, moments later adding that he thought his left leg (which was tangled in the bike and appeared unharmed) was in pain and possibly broken.

He knew his name, and said that he was just in shock. Someone asked me for my information (name, driver's license number, etc.) and put the paper with the scrawled numbers into his backpack. I parked my car in the lot out of the way of the entrance. No one dared to move the victim, not even to disengage him from the web of the bike; the security guard from the alley stood sentinel over him, making sure of this. He, quietly repeating to himself the words, *he—she—no one supposed to take your driver license number—I not supposed to take your driver license number—only the police supposed to do that.*

While I was exiting my vehicle just yards away in the parking lot, I was approached by a middle-aged woman wearing a man's tie and turning a slight limp off of her left leg, who told me she had been driving behind me, heading westbound on the boulevard at the same time. Further, she offered that she had seen the bicyclist "holding on to the back of the truck" for a distance of perhaps several blocks (east of the alley).

She used the phrases "hitching on the back'" and "tagging," and I noticed small remnants of spittle misting off of her too-wet mouth as she spoke there in the yellow light of the parking lot. She offered to give me her information and said she would be willing to present herself as a witness should I need her. I took down her number, placed it on the seat of my car, glanced at her for an imperceptible moment, and to myself, barely audible, asked her if she was a secretary, if she was employed.

Point Six: An Interruption in the Present Moment

Years ago, when I had visited the British pubs in northern Europe, things were noticeably different, though at once, exactly the same. The bars, tattooed on the inside with cigarette smoke and men in conversation, loud talk and liquor. Crowded around the pool table, they referred to the game as "spots and stripes," and not the conventional "stripes and solids" I was accustomed to hearing in the States.

Before each game between strangers, the house rules for the table were renegotiated, with parameters agreed upon for play. Before the game ever started, the battle had begun....

Charging down the stairwell of my apartment building earlier in the evening, before finding myself here in the parking lot of the bowling alley, I had neatly avoided a shameful catastrophe.

I am in the habit of rushing headlong down the four flights of stairs, all in a calculated effort to beat a timed record to the bottom floor of the lobby in one mad dash. My personal best currently stands at just under thirty-eight seconds. Rounding the stairs between the third and second floors, I very nearly tripped disastrously as I noticed something out of the very bottom of my sightline, twitching.

In the industrial gray of the utility carpet, something there seemed to stir, tucked in tightly between the crease in two stairs. Kneeling down, I came close enough to smell the stiffened cat, too scared to move, all gray stripes and neatly camouflaged. Having nearly killed the thing, I paused to stroke it lengthwise, over its bony ribcage, rubbing the tops of its back feet, long like that of a rabbit, satisfied at having restored its dignity once the gentle rumbling began to stir deep from within its throat. The trees, the citizen soldiers hidden in trees, the tanks slicing by, stroked along their sides with branches. In a flash, I was off again.

Point Seven: Distraction and Etymology (Waiting for Helen?)

From the parked car, I returned to the injured biker, whose name I then learned was Carl. He was now huddled into the concrete space near where the sidewalk drops down from the curb, all metal and limbs curled up like a half-man half-robot ampersand. Again, I asked him if there was anything he needed, if there was someone whom he wanted to call, and after muttering a name that sounded something like "Ellen," he quietly said no. From somewhere in the night, sirens wailed.

"Do you know what posh means?"

"What?"

"Don't think about your leg. Posh. Do you know what it means?"

"Ah—upper-crusty? Something like that?"

"No, not like the dictionary definition."

"Then no."

"Means *Port Outward, Starboard Home.* It's an old nautical term. Comes from the British navy. I guess they had nothing to do, you know, just a bunch of old geezers out on a boat together in the middle of nowhere for months on end."

"Crazy."

"So it does mean elegant. You were right about that. But really, where it comes from is nautical. Legend? I don't know. Story goes that wealthy British passengers preferred the more expensive, shady cabins on the port side of the ships going out through the Mediterranean on their way to India, and on the starboard side returning to Britain."

"That's nice. Did somebody call the ambulance yet? I think I'm going into shock."

"Do you know where the phrase, 'someone let the cat out of the bag' comes from?

"'Cause it's nautical, too?"

When the fire department finally showed up to remove the bike from around the leg, and check his vitals, neck and back, he was nearly passed out and shivering violently.

By this time, I had explained to him the nautical origins for "chew the fat," "loose cannon," "freezing the balls off a brass monkey" and a dozen others I made up right there on the spot. The paramedic swiftly dislodged the leg from inside the frame of the bicycle, in two or three separate, violent motions. Another paramedic was checking his pulse, pushing down into his chest, causing him to wince. I stood several feet away from all this, alone on the sidewalk, closer than anyone else, looking down at the scene. My jacket was in a bundle next to the bike, and I supposed for an instant that anyone looking on from the parking lot behind me could clearly see the letters "WED" spelling out the day of the week across my back, visible now through the collared white over-shirt.

I stared intensely, wondering if I was a criminal or an idiot, or somehow a victim myself, partially divorced as I was from reality. I could see every meal in every diner as I would work my way across the continent by bus, by rental car, by assumed name. The paramedics examined his leg to see if it was broken, squeezed it, pulled off his black shoe and sock, barked at him to curl his toes. I stared and stared down at his foot, knowing full well that indeed, he was not the *real* victim here.

At that moment, I realized that this was still about me, that the corporate bureaucracy indoors, now bowling and waiting for my arrival, for cannon fodder, was powerful enough to orchestrate just such an event, *to thoroughly and mockingly thrust my face in it.*

They had done everything possible to draw me closer to them—away from myself—to force me to ponder how the accident might one day expose me, and thusly, with sock removed beneath the forceful commands to curl my toes—show my spot to the world. The world was no longer a place of relative safety, secured by perpetual anonymity; I could no longer hide behind stripes. I hung my head in shame.

At 11:05 that night, I called the hospital and asked after the bike rider, Carl. Though the receptionist in the emergency room said she could not give out information over the phone, I told her I had gotten into an accident with a bike rider, and was curious to know how he was doing. She said that "he was there and he was stable" and could say no more. I confirmed this with her, trying desperately to explain away my culpability, my guilt.

"We are—all of us—put on the earth only to play host to vulnerability: it is a parasite that owns and binds us all," I whimpered into the phone. There was nothing on the other end of the line. Silently, I hung up.

PART TWO

NAGASAKI & WHAT NOT: POST-TRAUMATIC DREAMSCAPES

THE DEAD MAN

The man who lives in the house across the street from me—soon he is going to die. Do you want to know how I know? I went down to the sidewalk to see if the mail had come yet (this is the one daily chore around the house that I actually like to do), and a woman's voice echoed from across the street, up to the hill where we live. The echo on this street is amazing; it's like yelling into the bottom of a metal trash can, almost. For a future CIA agent, echoes represent genius: you get to overhear something from afar, while no one can see you listening. I heard the dying man's wife talking to a friend of hers on the telephone, as she stood out on the driveway just in front of their two-car garage: this was the source of the echo. She sounded like something close to a broken radio at first, standing with her back facing me, her voice static-y and shrill. As she turned around to face in my direction, though, I made out the following important words: ...*planning for a funeral this way, it really is an unbearable ending....*

Unlike most people's houses out here in the suburbs, their garage is always empty, which I think added to the volume of the echo. On the telephone, she was telling whomever she was talking to at the time that her husband was about to die. *This can't go on much longer —I think the end is near, sweetheart....* The small toy poodle named Ark was trembling, and cringed in a corner on top of the washer dryer unit, afraid it might get wet. I couldn't tell from where I was standing if Ark was shaking out of fear or if the washing machine was in its final spin cycle. Counted among my least favorite chores around the house: doing my own laundry. She had the cordless phone in her left hand and the garden hose in her right, hosing the cement off and talking. She very nearly tripped over the *flaccid* hose, kinked and twisted in several places, yanking it up in between her legs while struggling to work both the phone and the chore she was attending to. I say flaccid because I have to—it's my homework, and not an easy word to work into normal talking. That lady must hose down the garage floor and driveway at least nineteen times a day. She told her friend on the phone that the dying man had brain cancer, or maybe I just thought that's what she said, and I actually heard the rumor from some other neighbor down the block. Either way it made me mad, her just standing there for the whole neighborhood to overhear, in her salmon pink tank top and mom shorts. You know how much people talk in neighborhoods—it's tough to get a bit of privacy with all the loose-lipped ladies *pontificating* on about things. (That was another of my homework words.) And the kids listen to it. All of it. Maybe everybody's just bored with their own lives and wanting to peek into everyone else's. The real heart of the matter is that if I'm not the only one holding the information, or *intelligence*, as the CIA might refer to it, then the information isn't really all that valuable.

Her husband sells cardboard boxes for a living. When the garage door is up and the floor is dry, he can be seen folding boxes of various sizes into perfect cubes, bottom first and then the top, after which he takes the whole thing back apart and throws it onto the bed of the truck that's parked out front. Then he disappears for hours. I've thought about calling over there before, mostly after he disappears, to tell the woman not to tell so many of her friends about her husband. I think about telling her that death is much too private a thing to be gabbing about on the phone in the middle of the street, but I think my anonymous status is much more important than anything I might be able to tell her directly. *Anonymity* is a word I could practice on her. So is *phlebotomy*, which means bloodletting. Maybe I should write her a note and stick it in her mailbox: *Stop telling everyone about the dying man: don't make me have to cut you.* I could write it with my left hand instead of my right, the perfect way to mask the handwriting's true source. She would never, ever know it was from me.

Mac and cheese always seems exactly like what astronaut food should be to me, and I am always craving it. Ever since I was ten, I like it best when it gets squishy. Every time you try to stab a fork-full of the little macaroni elbows, that wet plastic noise talks back to you from the bowl. Smells like plastic, too. Yellow plastic food, tasting weirdly like metal and mustard mixed together, only really good.

We're out of mac and cheese now at my house, and I have to go to the market to load up on my supply. If we run out of mac and cheese, I wind up coming down with a cold in about two or three days. No one in my family can figure it out. Mom sends me to the store to re-supply the cupboard because I can almost drive by myself now, and I guess she figures the market is only two blocks away and on small neighborhood streets with not very much traffic. *And* with the exception of the time when I crashed into the nursery tree lot right by the entrance to the freeway last month, my driving record is still perfect, which should make me a shoo-in for acceptance to the CIA one day. My friend Jones and I were drinking brand new cherry Slurpees from the 7-11 on Trinity Avenue when I crashed through the cyclone fence and into a giant sycamore, so when the police came to the scene to make out reports, everything in the car (including me and Jones), looked like it was covered in blood. If we hadn't been laughing so hard, I'm pretty sure we could have made the six o'clock local news for a minute, because when the police first pulled up, they were looking like they were gonna' draw their guns on us. Maybe they thought we'd been hideously bludgeoning old moms in the neighborhood to death, trying to formulate a secret zombie army, but then their training kicked in and they realized we were just drinking Slurpees.

I'm at the market when I see the dying man pushing his cart in front of me in the aisle with the cake mixes and cereal boxes, and I am hardly surprised. He is my neighbor, after all, and even though we live near a big city, we are still in the suburbs, where things are laid out pretty neatly with houses nearby parks, markets and other important stores. Neighbors have to eat, too, and this is the market that's closest to everyone on my street. We've never really formally met before, so I'm pretty sure he doesn't know who I am and there's no danger of being caught spying on him. I'm just another person in the market, pushing my cart around in the same aisle as him. Besides that, he's dying and has much more important things worth paying attention to. The cart he is pushing only has a few things in it: seedless red grapes, a box of toothpicks with the little colored hats on one end, a can of mixed nuts, nonfat milk, fruit yogurt that I can't see the label of, tortilla chips (round), and a piece of fish in a plastic bag that smells like my cat's tongue from here. His cart is pulling to the right a lot, and from eight feet away, I can see him struggling to keep it in the path where it won't hit any oncoming traffic.

Sometimes I like to pretend that my cart is pulling one way, and when a woman is bending over to pull something off the shelf in front of her, maybe a jar of Best Foods mayonnaise or Mott's cinnamon swirl apple sauce, I'll accidentally swerve the cart close by her butt. When the back of my hand rubs her behind, I'll apologize and explain, "Sorry, lady, but my cart keeps pulling to the right." I wonder to myself if the dying man is thinking that he doesn't deserve to be pushing around a cart that pulls him away from the straight path down the aisle. My English teacher at school would probably insist there's a metaphor in there somewhere, but I don't know. Sure—he's dying, and there's a path in life that leads in a pretty curvy way to that, so maybe it's actually better if he doesn't go straight because they say the closest distance between two points is a straight line. Should I tell him about the butt trick so he can use it? I wonder about the *adroitness* of someone who is dying. Like I said, they might have too much on their minds already. Or maybe he thinks that he has enough to deal with as it is. After all, he's dying.

My teacher tries to make everyone in the class use our vocab words in real life for homework, so that should explain my way. Here's another try: The fluorescent lights in the grocery store hum *sub-audibly* like an enormous chorus of tiny insects. You can hear them especially well when you hit the frozen foods section, where I make sure to throw a box of Neapolitan ice cream sandwiches into the cart. Vanilla, chocolate and pink. The dying man is deciding which brand of corn dogs he should buy, and I need them too, so I have to wait by the green peas before I can get my own. He's casual, maybe too casual, which is *augmented* by the fact that his clothes are ill-fitting, too big, like a tee shirt you wear into the swimming pool. I'm happy he's left the house in a windbreaker, which is burgundy, because the last thing I want is for him to get even more sick standing this long in front of the open freezer door. He most likely doesn't realize that if you rub the sacks of frozen peas around in your hand, they feel like a bunch of hardened bird eyes, which is what I am investigating while I wait for him to make his dying mind up.

With the freezer door open, the inside of the glass starts to fog up in front of the dying man. Can a dying man even eat a corn dog? I bet that's the only way that a corn dog could actually taste any better: knowing that every bite might be your last bite of corn dog, forever and ever, amen. Maybe he's picking out the taster menu for his own funeral services—like they'll serve corndogs and mac and cheese and strawberry-filled Pop Tarts with white frosting and sprinkles in light of his untimely demise. I should be so lucky, but I know that's what I'd do. Tonight, when I get home and Mom cooks corn dogs for my dinner, I'm going to pretend like I am dying too, and savor each and every bite of my corn dog like it's my last. Corn dogs taste best with mustard and some beer that I sneak from Dad when Mom goes to get some extra napkins from the pantry. Mustard is yellow, too, but not the same yellow as my mac and cheese. Or my hair, for that matter. One is yellow that's closer to green, one is yellow that's closer to orange, and one is yellow that's closer to white. Mustard stains my hands when I eat corn dogs, and I look like I have jaundice of the fingers, or something. At least that's what my biology teacher says. Can a person die from jaundice?

The dying man is in the *nine items or less* line at the checkout stand, and I am two people behind him, reading the tiny horoscope booklet disinterestedly, because in actuality, I'm really counting how many items the dying man is placing on the conveyer belt. If a person puts more than nine items on there, I get really pissed and wish to myself first that they would run into another car in the parking lot on their way out, and second, that I get to see it if it happens. A collision is technically defined as *violent forcible contact between two or more things,* and I like them. A lot. You might say this little fascination of mine is *preternatural,* or even *aberrant.* I certainly would. But I just ended up this way, so what could I do? I count eleven items in front of the dying man, and I have to decide very quickly not to blow the whistle on him because I may blow my cover at the same time. It's not like it's a spy mission that I am on, but it can't hurt to be prepared to join the CIA with some finely tuned skills in covert ops. At least that's what I always say. Besides my not wanting to rat him out to the cashier and everyone else in line, he's dying already, and maybe if I wish that he hits another car in the parking lot, it might jinx something and he could wind up dying before it's time, or even running the car into me before he crashes. And the truth is, I like the dying man. With all those boxes he's got, he's an essay in organization—a well-ordered man trying desperately to bring order to a chaotic universe, one cardboard packing box at a time. Just like the CIA, except without guns. Maybe I even see myself in the dying man, a little bit.

The lady at the checkout stand is named Brenda. It says so on the little tag thingy on her vest, which is dark brown-red like dried blood. No one gets named Brenda anymore. Judging by the way she looks, which to me resembles a really old coat that my great aunt pulls out of the closet when it gets too cold (scrunched up, furry and kind of worn, like the mold that attacks the old fruit on the counter at home), she may well have been the last one ever to get the name. She doesn't say anything but, "Hell-ooh, how are you today," with a tiny Texas accent that stays bubbly from beginning to end. I guess she decided not to blow the whistle on the dying man, either. Thirty seconds later and he's walking out the door, and now it's my turn because the lady in front of me only had a carton of cigarettes, and I rush my hello to Brenda because I want to see what the dying man is going to do next. I have to hurry up and get out to the parking lot where I can continue to conduct my *surveillance*. Four boxes of Kraft mac and cheese, one box of Neapolitan ice cream sandwiches, three boxes of corn dogs, and a bottle of French's regular yellow mustard is nine items, and I am out of there just as the dying man is finishing loading up his car.

Out of the parking lot, there is no choice but to drive home together, my car pretty close behind, though I try to hide myself as best I can by actively letting anyone get in front of me during the few short blocks on the way back home. I probably should have tried harder to get in front of him, which would have been the best option—to play the leader while still technically following his every move. Now I'm not that good at math, but if my neighbor was *one* and the dying man (her husband) was *two*, that would make me technically a "disinterested *third* party" like they're always saying on the crime shows I watch on television. Only I can't really stop spying on the dying man across the street. Partly because it's my mission to practice paying close attention to everything around me that seems out of the ordinary, and partly because he's the sympathetic character in my life's narrative. I tell Mom that the cancer I heard he has must feel like someone building huge cardboard boxes inside the dying man's head and then breaking them down again, over and over. She tells me I've got quite an imagination, and that dying is not something to be made fun of. After the market, the dying man returns home to eat, I guess, because his car is next to the truck in the driveway over there. I wonder to myself if they maybe had corn dogs for dinner tonight. Dying people have to eat too, after all, and when there's something in the world as good as corn dogs and mustard, who could blame the dying man for a little *indulgence*? That's my newest vocabulary word, in case you didn't know. Homework: finished.

POLAROID FAMILY PORTRAITURE

My mother doesn't know that I know about the broken statues. Or if she does know, at least we never talk about it. The silvery-gray cloud of emulsion misted in and out of focus, as lines formed and the story of a chalky white garden statue slowly came into frame. The thin white lines of the Polaroid marked the edges, and the leafy green layers of foliage defined the picture. My mother only ever bought the broken ones. This is a fact that I recently discovered while on a joint venture to the local nursery.

It could be said that this tiny version of a photograph is a kind of detail. The information is limited in scale to around three inches square, but for as small an area as this is, in most cases, that is all one needs to get an idea of the story being told.

She rifled through the little cemeteries of cement-gray animals on the ground, shaded by the ferns overhead and the gridded mesh pattern of the screen on the patio at the nursery. They looked sad, sitting there: frozen in time, tiny victims of an invisible Medusa, only not really anxious to escape their stillness, just calm. She never paid attention to the nice ones. The dog with the broken tail looked better to her; I could tell she was eyeing it. She scooped it up, much like a person would scoop up a real puppy, tenderly. This was the one she would buy.

The drive home was short, in reality less than twenty minutes, though it seemed to last over an hour. We spoke not more than a few words each, and for whatever reason, we kept the radio off, opting instead to listen to the noise the wind makes with all of the car windows down. When we got home, we unloaded the car quietly. My mother seemed intently focused as I lifted the heavy bags of gravel out of the trunk of the car. Dust and dry silt sifted out of a tiny rip in the seam of the bag, making a dusty trail along the gray slate of the garage floor and out to the backyard. I watched to see what she would do with the little doggy, how she would go about mending this broken lump of cement, where she would retire this sad little animal. She, standing there for a moment, in a mesh, floppy, wood-colored garden hat, white shirt and an old pair of jeans. The new junipers angled out of the back seat windows, too tall and proud to fit inside completely, and I had to lean into the car, fit my hands around the black plastic pot, and straight-back the whole thing up and out of the window. I could see her out of the corner of my eye just then, picking up the yellow plastic bag that covered the doggy statue. I don't think she noticed I was watching her.

The line of things from the nursery extended along the edge of the patio, which bordered the grassy area and separated the barbecue from everything else. Twelve bags of gravel in two piles of six; three new California junipers now standing military-style with feathery but hard green plumes extending upward all in one motion; two one-gallon jugs of Vitamin B-12 for added strength in new plant growth; some tiny blue Lobelia flowers to edge the garden in with a thin yet electric line of color; a new rose bush in a five-gallon pot to complement the rest of the roses; a flat of some alien-looking ground cover named Bugleweed or *Ajuga reptans* (it said on the label), the kind that looks like a humongous dinner salad is taking over the garden while you're planting it in the ground, eclipsing most everything else around it in seconds. And then there was the doggy statue, sans tail, lying there at the end of the line, still in the yellow plastic bag.

She was careful to acknowledge that it was indeed a part of the loot from the nursery adventure, as she placed it in the row at the end, off by itself, looking quite regal there in its golden yellow bag. The edges of the bag were tightly turned over several times, and formed what looked like a soft velvety cushion underneath the doggy statue.

I told her I had to go to the bathroom, hoping she would believe me and get to work placing the statue somewhere out in the yard. I ran into the house, slamming the back door behind me. From the window in my bedroom on the second floor, I could see out over the backyard. Sure enough, there she was, hunched over and bent at the knees, resting in a little pile at the edge of the lawn. She had the statue in her hands, if only for another few seconds before she found a resting place beneath the drooping trees along the border of the property.

I saw her dig out a little mound with her right hand somewhere next to the rose garden and behind the rocks at the very edge of the lawn. She held the doggy in her left hand as she scratched out the dirt with the other in curving motions imitating a capital "C," moving the dirt towards her and then off to the right. She patted down the newly exposed section, and slowly placed the doggy in its new bed. I had caught her in the act. I would keep quiet about it, though, and returned to the backyard minutes later, pretending as if nothing had happened.

She was no longer out by the doggy. She was standing next to the junipers, asking me to go ahead and plant them in a row of three at the corner of the yard. They would make a nice little shield from the neighbors behind us, and I started to dig the three holes in the place she had selected, taking the rest of the afternoon to complete the task of restoring the plants to the earth, in their new home, our backyard.

Days later I noticed that the flat of ground cover was entirely planted in the three feet of space around the statue. The fact that this was entirely too much ground cover to locate in a space this small was something that could not have escaped even the most amateur of gardeners, much less someone with as green a thumb as my mother. In fact, an entire flat of any kind of ground cover could be planted over ten times as much area as that. Especially this kind of ground cover, the kind that had practically surrounded the little doggy statue in just the three days since it came to lie there.

I knelt down in front of the statue. Leaning over slightly, I looked at it like an altar boy might look at the tabernacle behind the heavy marble bench the priests always sat on, eyeing it up and down, side to side. It was weird. The ground cover crept in around it on all four sides, approaching the place near its rear where the tail once was, somehow appearing to heal over the wound like a gauze wrap or a band-aid made only of green, organic matter. I turned it a little to the left, moving it backwards towards the ground cover that was most promising of quick growth, encouraging the healing process to begin. I felt like Neosporin ointment, helping out like that.

I took the Polaroid camera from where it rested on both my legs. The cord around my neck kept the thing from falling over into the dirt or the plants. I opened her up and waited patiently for the green "ready" light to come on. Looking cautiously around me one more time, I leaned in to the statue again, even closer this time, and snapped the portrait of the little doggy. I begged him to smile secretly for the camera, but nothing. I watched the grays shifting in and out, different lines roughing out the contours in the picture, eagerly awaiting the details of this strange family portrait, a picture I might one day reveal to my own children, a secret way of knowing their long-lost grandmother.

RECENT EPISODES IN AN EVER-EXPANDING BIRDLAND

Scenario One

There is a boy. He is a boy enrolled in a college somewhere in the Midwest, probably a public university, probably the University of Minnesota, or perhaps even Missouri State University. This boy believes that he is in love with the girl on the fourth floor, the floor above his own, in the dorm where he has spent the first of nine months in his second year of university. In the dorm room: a collection of ferns, withering sadly. (Boy, dropped as a child, rolling end over end down the curving staircase like a foul ball, landing in a crescent shape, four limbs gathered together, near the crack underneath the front door, a whispering chilled breeze sweeping over his cheeks). Although he has never seen the face of the girl, he is convinced that the nightly *klip...klop...klip* of the high-heeled shoes on the ceiling above his bed is a detail from a nightly story he is being told from above. It is paraphrased in a personal Morse code, then hand-delivered from her beloved's soles to his ears. The tapping registers faster on Wednesdays: she is frantically pecking out love poems; there are scuffles and muted drags every Friday: she prepares him a favorite meal, chicken fricassee and perhaps a double baked mashed potato with the insides removed and then returned to the peel. (When the boy was ten, he was taken on a visit to a trauma Crisis Center in his hometown, probably somewhere in New Jersey or even Philadelphia, and since then, he believes that Las Vegas is in the process of taking over the entire country, and possibly the whole world. Cited as evidence, Indian gaming casinos popping up everywhere: Indio, California; Tuscaloosa, Wyoming; Tupelo, Mississippi. Cited as evidence, cleaner air being pumped into the atmosphere, making him feel healthier, making him stay awake longer. Cited as evidence, new dollar bills, more like play money than the bills before. Cited as evidence, his inexplicable fondness for hotels). When he decided that this was indeed true, he immediately went to the local sewing-slash-fabric store and purchased the strongest adhesive-backed Velcro that his money could buy, and returned to the dorm room, saying hello to his ferns, weeping. He proceeded to Velcro all of his remote controls to the wall next to his bunk bed, lining them up in a row of four, organized by height from tallest to shortest. For about a half an hour that day, he felt better, and crawled up to his roomie's bunk to prepare for the footsteps that evening.

Scenario Two

A man named Pete runs the quality control office for the graveyard shift in the department of Negative Assembly in the number two film processing company in the city of Hollywood, California. Pete plays the "eagle" to the rest of these wide-eyed "night owls." He is the second in command, though at times, it would seem to his fellow workers that he is the only one in charge of the entire company between the hours of ten thirty p.m. and six in the morning. (When a person makes the daily regimen of life take place when the body's natural biorhythms demand sleep and darkness, strange things seep out of the personality like gray-green goo from an open sore). If he overhears his co-workers talking about a newly purchased 1960 black Chevy Impala sitting in the parking lot of the film lab, Pete jumps in and offers everything there is to know about the Chevrolet line of automobiles, including that he was born in the backseat of a 1950 Chevrolet, and instead of a pacifier, he was given a monkey wrench to suck on as a baby. (The metal taste in his mouth makes him think of war, the years that his father spent away from home, engaged in battle overseas; certainly he was not a general leading thousands of men to their deaths, Pete. Perhaps he was just an ordinary soldier, an enlisted soldier, Pete). One day, he asks a co-worker if he likes his new haircut, which is a buzz. The man says sure, now that it's summer, the short hair will be nice to have in the heat (which has begun to blanket the surrounding hills of Hollywood, sticking to every living thing the way leg flesh sticks to the vinyl car seat). Pete begins to tell the man that he shaved his own head with a set of clippers that he recently purchased from a large wholesale membership type of club. He removes his wallet from his front left pocket, offering the platinum membership card as proof that he indeed belongs to the club, and moves in the circles of upper echelon wholesale warehouse club membership. He continues, unprovoked, telling the man that the clippers that he is using now can't hold a candle to the clippers he owned as a youth, when he managed to go through about two or three sets in a period of seven years. He tells the man that the clippers he used to shave his head with as a youth could cut through the hair of ten or twelve small dogs at a time, and come out the other end of the job virtually unscathed. Try to get that done with the clippers they're offering out there on the market nowadays.

Scenario Three

A boy in Worcester, Massachusetts, grows up in a home that is perpetually smelly. If you've ever lived on top of a sulfur mine, then you know what I'm talking about: the kind of smell that opens up the nostrils, and won't let go. Rotten eggs housed in old sweatsocks. The boy's father, Turk, shovels animal feces at the Boston Zoo, alternating weekly with another man named Earl between the gorilla and the big cat cages. Turk fingers a constant rhythm with his left hand along the wooden stem of the shovel, one-two-three, one-two-three, but no one seems to notice. One night the boy has a dream about his father, the setting of which takes place in the old west of books he likes to read from the public library. He has never seen a movie with a brown-haired actor that he enjoyed. The boy respects his father very greatly, but wishes that he could convince him to get into a four-way duel with the actors Andie MacDowell, Bill Pullman and Keanu Reeves, the way the scenario occurs in the dream he has now had on more than one occasion. The four line up in a cross formation, MacDowell facing Reeves, his father facing Pullman, each with two celery sticks drawn from leather holsters on their hips, one pointed at the person in front, and one pointed at the person to the right. At night, he closes his eyes before he goes to sleep, and says a little prayer, asking God to deliver his father into the landscape of his four-way gun-fighting picture, only this time, with a real gun. Chickens run around free all about the old western town in the dream, pecking out little orders to the gunslingers in the duel, frozen stiff with celery sticks drawn. In the dream, Earl owns the saloon out of which each of the gunslingers has stepped, slamming down shot glasses of brand-less whiskey before dismounting rickety stools and pushing through the swinging doors into the plaza. Eight cowboy boots going *klip...klop...klip* lazily in unison across the old wooden floor of the saloon. In real life, Earl is the man from the northern part of the city who bought two peacocks and let them run free in his front yard until the two eventually mated, producing several offspring that he let roam freely around the streets of the neighborhood. One of the peacocks was named Michael. After a few years in the neighborhood, the man noticed that several other fowl were mysteriously appearing in the front yard of his property. Ducks, owls, chickens, finches and other waterfowl paraded noisily around and on top of the small fountain that he placed there as a bathtub for the birds. Blue jays patrolled from high atop the pepper trees, dive-bombing the Venus in the middle of the fountain, prison guards in uniform. Regularly, the peacocks fanned out their tail feathers gracefully in the middle of the street, only to be leveled by a passing car. The bird was all fluff. What amounted to about a bowling ball-sized mass of guts was anchored to the ground with tiny foot-tall legs, skinny. Tail plumage extending out in a half circle whose radius was about as wide as an average man is tall, covering sloppy windshields on contact, only to be wiped off with the same arcing motion of the wiper blades. Fines were issued to such motorists, to the tune of one thousand dollars, by the chubby policemen in the town. At first Earl was angry at the birds in his front yard. Later he was not angry. Then he was happy. Waterfowl.

Scenario Four

Gerald and Phil are sitting in an Indian Gaming Casino at the outskirts of the Hopi Indian Facility in Indio, California. Recent funds have been earmarked for the facility, in the hopes of converting the termite-style tent into a real building, perhaps one made of adobe. Each man has a mere five dollars to his name, the bills burning small fires in their respective pockets. At the blackjack table in the casino, sitting in the third base position, Gerald begins to tell the story of his childhood day camp, and the boy with the sharpened kitty-style teeth who would never say anything besides the words, "Noivuss, koivuss," to anyone who came within a few feet of him. At first, he thought the kid was retarded: the day they made lamps out of papier-mâché, he remembers how difficult it was for him to blow up the balloon. Then when the day came that they had to learn how to feed the fish, he couldn't turn the fish food container over slowly enough to do anything but empty the entire container of flakes out onto the carpet. The chicken coop in the play yard at the camp housed two chickens named Pedro and Inez. During finger-painting lessons, the kid always left the class and locked himself in the cage, hoisting Pedro onto his lap for a severely rough petting session involving blue crayons and damp paper towels. He continued to tell the story, offering toward the end that it was in this day camp that he first started hating celery and peanut butter, and that if anyone there thought they were going to force him to eat the stuff, they would have another thing coming. The dealer thought that the two men had better leave the table, and because they weren't betting anything, the pit boss also felt that it was their time to go. On their way out of the door, Phil took the opportunity to tell Gerald that he quite enjoyed his story about the day camp, and that if he ever found himself in a fighting mood, he would like to try his hand at forcing a little celery down Gerald's throat. He noticed that Gerald had broken a slight sweat on his forehead, and had begun to look a little nervous as they approached the door to leave the casino. He took out his brown bi-fold wallet, and handed it over to Phil, saying with a hint of sadness in his voice, "I bought this so you could have it. I thought you would need it, and so I bought it." Moral to the story: never look a gift bi-fold in the mouth.

Scenario Five

Gervase (hard 'g'), Gervase is a boy whose friends all believe is in love with his sister, who lives somewhere back in the central states, though he has never told any of his friends exactly where. His best friend is named Bear, and not because this is a nickname, either, but because this is his actual last name. Some of the group claim that they have seen Bear before, wearing a very short, shimmery silver lamé dress. Michael is the outspoken "nickname-giver" of the group, and one day realizes that Gervase does not have a nickname. Obsessed with the superhero situation, he decides that Gervase's nickname should aspire to superhero levels, if this is indeed possible. Browsing through an art magazine of some repute in the local coffee shop, Michael comes upon an advertisement for an upcoming show. In the advertisement is a close-up photo of a Taxidermied snow-white owl, complete with mysterious orange-gold eyes. Shortly after, Michael names Gervase "Roni Horn's the Owl," encouraging the others in the group to notice the distinct superhero nature of the nickname. It is at this time he cites the story that Gervase told them once about his cousin who was born with a small tail just below the belt-line of his pants, and how the doctors left it on him instead of cutting it off, offering this story in defense of the superhero nature of the nickname. Perhaps Roni Horn's the Owl has birds in his family; even cousins can be good for something. Halloween arrives, and Michael and Roni Horn's the Owl decide to team up for their costume, donning an outfit they title, "Siamese Twins Attached at the Penis." Each boy wears a similarly checked light blue short-sleeve shirt with an industrial gray long-sleeve underwear top underneath, sneakers and a pair of ordinary blue jeans. Hours before the festivities begin, the two boys relentlessly cut off the legs of several used Levi's, halving each leg lengthwise and sewing it back together into a tube shape. After stuffing each four-foot denim tube with old crumpled newspaper, they sew eight tubes together, creating a nearly thirty-foot-long denim penis, which they each attach by way of safety pins to the inside of their button flies, creating the connection that Siamese twins all depend on for their status. Policemen ask them what their costume is supposed to be, requesting that they please kindly remove the urine-filled zip-lock baggies tied to their belts with plastic ribbon, offering in addition, "We don't care that you insist it's only lemonade, thank you." Siamese twins attached at the penis have to wear colostomy bags on their hips, hanging there like Superman's *kryptonite*, an "Achilles Bladder" of sorts. Later in the evening, the Siamese twins locate among the thousands of costumed people gathered in the plaza, four superheroes and one midget dressed as a tiny green leprechaun. Posing for perhaps the most notable picture of the evening in all Halloween history in the city, the Siamese twins separate, extending the length of the penis they share to its thirty-some-odd-foot capacity, and bookend the four superheroes and leprechaun. Featuring them assembled in a line from left to right with twelve hands holding up the denim penis, the photos that end up in hundreds of strangers' picture books read: Roni Horn's the Owl, Captain America,

Daredevil, Leprechaun, Green Lantern, Aquaman and Michael. Careful, leprechauns are known to bite ankles on buses.

I DREAM OF AFRICA

One morning I awoke with the strange idea that the dream I just had in my sleep was, in reality, a memory from my childhood. My father was an equitable, righteous and celebrated older man whose notoriously hideous relationship with my mother was the subject of gossip in areas surrounding our estate for miles. He kept a farm that housed several hundred head of cattle, and the required help to maintain the grounds, the house and the herd. South Africa was a strange place to live in the seventies, apartheid being in full swing, although, as a little boy, I hardly realized what was going on, being so remote from the majority of civilization while on that ranch.

I used to sit in a bundle on the hard, square marble tiles in the foyer, licking the cold surface with the tip of my tongue until one of the servants would pluck me up off the ground and return me to the nursery. I never ate carrots, and at the age of seven, would take wild rides in the afternoon on the backs of our pet ostriches, assisted in the mounting of the birds by my father, whose wild chuckling and two missing fingers were fodder for nearly every servant's late-night mocking.

Of course they didn't let him hear them making fun of him. Surely it was all in jest, though, as you could tell from their smiles how they loved him so. The legend among the house servants had it that my father's first assistant several years before I was born was helping him out in the wood shed with a peculiar carpentry project one balmy spring night. My father had gotten it into his head to construct a large wooden goat out of aged black Bubinga wood, and had thus procured the help of Linnus, a graceful little fifteen-year old from a neighboring village whom my father had rescued from a horrible fate in a local traveling circus because of his severely mangled left leg, now much shorter than his right.

As it turned out, Linnus *was* graceful to a fault, but proved worthless with the hammer. Holding the tail on the back end of the goat firmly, my father urged Linnus to pound the nail home steadily into the wood, as he motioned for him to pick up the nail and the hammer. Linnus was overjoyed and hurriedly clutched at the hammer, leaning hard into his good right foot for extra balance. Luck had it that Linnus was an awful shot, had never even *seen* a hammer before, and drove the nail clean through my father's left hand, missing all of the major ligaments and bones, but thoroughly fastening his hand to the goat's ass.

Apparently, my father was in such pain that he subsequently bit off the index and middle finger on his "good" hand, just to avoid screaming bloody murder, waking everyone on the farm, and scaring the now sheet-white Linnus off into the Kalahari desert. Legend also had it my father played a mean backgammon in those days.

The large birds would gallop delightfully around the grounds, craning their ostrich necks gracefully back and forth, sometimes getting up to speeds of around twelve miles an hour. My hands were small, and though I remember gripping their sweaty necks with all my strength, I would still occasionally get thrown, always tumbling off to one side or the other with my father rushing over to the scene of the accident.

At night, I would stay up as late as I could, leaning in behind my father's shoulder at the poker table in the snooker room, drowsy from all the little sips of brandy he allowed me to steal. Sometimes my mother would come 'round, mostly after a fight with one of her several younger lovers, none of whom I ever actually saw, and whisk me off to bed. Later that year, when I was almost eight, she took off to Paris with two of my older brothers, and I never heard from her again.

NIGHT PITIES NEITHER MEN NOR

Yesterday, on the freeway, he saw a pigeon fly beneath a sport utility vehicle. Feathers spit out from beneath three sides of the undercarriage of the automobile, riding along in the slow lane of the freeway, billowing upwards in an attempt to escape from their very nature. Feathers flying on their own. He imagined three cake makers in a small factory somewhere, St. Louis maybe, erupting in laughter at the fallen wedding cake, saying "the hell with it," and breaking into a food fight with frosting lobbed back and forth, back and forth, flying, like feathers. Sharing the witness of the slain bird with road construction crews along the side of the freeway, he wondered what they would do with the carcass, what stories they would tell, if they ever found the head of the pigeon. All this in the span of a few seconds; he was a changed man.

> *I'm not sure what it is, really, but in finding myself in the mirror, something happens, something not unlike the feeling that washes over someone who has recently ingested a powerful pain killer, something vague and incomplete, something watery and fluid, and in this exchange with the other figure, myself, there is a special system of signs that is shared, and it is shared by only the two of us....*

It was a mission, in reality, that he was on. There was a place, although he had never been there, from which he was currently lost, a place to which he desperately wished to return. One evening at a local comedy club, a comedian told him that John Denver was the only man whom he idolized. John Denver, the man who came back from a sniper's position in the United States Army during the Vietnam War with one hundred and forty-seven recorded kills, more murders than hit songs, and this comedian may be the only person in the country with this murderous vision of Colorado John Denver, victim of a senseless plane crash somewhere over one of the landlocked square states. He asked this comedian for directions, thinking perhaps he was equally as lost as him, but spitting into his vodka from several feet away, he replied only with swaying and leaning, swaying and leaning.

This man has nothing to do with taxi cab drivers, with heads of state, with candy store owners. Never before has he seen as many stray dogs as the time he visited Mexico City in early summer four years ago. The secret language that stray dogs share, even more stylized than normal dog-speak, he thought.

I think that these noises, the ones that I might hear when simply walking down the street, or standing in front of the deli case in the meat market, it is these noises that come the closest of all language to talking about who I am. The squishing that one pound of meat makes when nestled in next to another is like a simple greeting, but one of respect and appreciation: the meats are proud to be who they are, governed by purpose and declining states of grace. I walk past, and hear the rump roast say to the pork spare ribs, "I see the way you interact with your children, and it makes me proud to be meat." Although the sausage takes subtle insult to the compliment, he flushes full red, for he is meat, as well. This is like a description of me, a man, made of meat.

He decided one day while alone at the breakfast table eating cereal flakes, that people who operated in the extremes of language and discourse (superficially, that is) were the only people worth reacting to. From one aisle of the supermarket later that day, he overheard a woman say that an acting class she took in Las Vegas was the scariest thing she had ever done in her entire life, rattling on that the class was comprised of *real* actors, emphasis on the word *real*, and therefore, there was nothing but three days of emphatic screaming, lecherous mood swinging, and so on. He heard little of this, though, because the second he heard the woman use the hyperbole, he darted down the aisle of frozen foods, turned the corner sharply, and bolted for the woman in question, tackling her amidst a sea of crashing jars of apple sauce and bottled water, making initial violent contact, linebacker-style, then jerking himself up and making a total body hurl of action, lunatic flailing of limbs, toward and out the automatic front doors. He had to think to himself – was this really the fight for him?

Alterity is a concept that says within our makeup, there is a part that we can never know. The postmodern condition is tenuous at best. All efforts to construct a complete portrait of who we are, a mirror with no shards missing to reflect back to us an image with nothing left out, are hopeless. With any luck, the part that we can never know is something trivial, a quality that will never be missed. What would it mean if the part of us that we could never know was the part that was our *destiny*, the *blueprint* for all of our searches in life, the *total* purpose for being? The fact that this man would never know his special purpose in life was bad enough. The idea that this was the part of him that was missing from his portrait was incomprehensible. He was a goldfish in a fishbowl.

Brushing his teeth one morning, he looked hazily into the mirror before him; the white goo was smudged about his lower lip, curling in a ribbon of foam over his chin. He was forced to recollect the time in college when his roommate decided to try out a supposed basic Hollywood horror film magic trick; namely, that if you put gobs of toothpaste beneath the eyes, strange puffiness and tearing would be induced after a short while. He recalled the photos, detritus from the dorm room staging of the B-movie faux-slasher flick, blurry and overwhelming in the lens of the camera, smeared in white goo and fake blood, unnervingly and strangely psychotic. He spat into the sink and rinsed, spat and rinsed.

The noise of fountains, strangely marching on to some unspecified destiny, the idea that one might be always existing in the middle of things, with a past and a future extending out in either direction, but never reached, always in the middle. The fountains calmed him, their sourcebook of gurgling named him, made him think of baby diapers, of time lost, of infant drivel and wooden toys, of first bikes and skinned knees, of the story his mom told him about the bird attacking her as she rode her bike up the sidewalk in front of her house, of the first time she saw Hitchcock's *The Birds*. Riding on the bus from one side of town to the other, faces passed through like old books in the configuration of rainbirds, chick – chick – chick – chick – chick – thrrrrrrrrrrrrrrrrrrrr – chick – chick – chick, and on. Could he pick a man's pockets without him knowing it? How would he play it off, were he to be accused; could he say it was someone else, and say it with a straight face? He saw the construction cranes through the crack in the window. Four inches of harmony systems, longing to be free of gravity, he thought.

I am thinking of toys, of tiny boats and model airplanes, of electric trains and plastic telephones...I entered my house one day to find that all the furniture had been moved around, and yet – no one had been there to visit in weeks: not one serviceman, nor relative, for weeks. This became a game that I played with myself, and quite often, as well. I would pretend to be leaving the house for vacation one morning, and later that day, I would sneak back into my own house, rearrange the furniture, and then lock back up and go to the library downtown. Hiding out in the library was easy: no one checks at the end of the day, and they never think twice about people that they might see in there several days in a row. After two or three days of being away from home, to return was to experience a lapse in reality, because I could actually forget who had changed the furniture for a minute or two. This was fine the first ten or twelve times; then, I began to forget how the furniture was in the first place every time, and the game lost all its freshness, decaying into the everyday like so many other things.

Half-asleep one morning in the shower, rinsing the soap from between the cheeks of his ass, he was awakened by a noise like a thousand tiny termites in a legendary pile of wood, all wired with a thousand tiny microphones, which were all hooked up to a single high school public address system in a basketball gymnasium, whose amplifier was turned up to ten. He thought to himself, this is the sound that religion would make, were it to talk, and it was speaking right to him. Two minutes went by, and no matter that it was just the smoke detector complaining about the steam from the shower, because this was surely the beginning of a message. He fixed himself some toast.

Diary entry dated January 11th, some years ago—

On the Subject of Irrational Fears:

Fear of the sound, presence, and/or usage
of **electric can openers**;

Fear of walking near, around, and especially
over **manhole covers**;

Fear of approaching or dining in a restaurant
that employs a **buffet style** of **dining**.

At night he had recurring dreams, always in black and white, of a man not unlike himself, who was either

constantly running down parking lot stairs or being
viewed from outside the elevator doors as he perpetually
rode up and down in a large metropolitan hotel. All this to
further himself from himself: there was no book of dreams
willing to take on such an interpretation; there was no
metaphor great enough to envelope his questions. Arms
clasped around his folded knees, he was locked in the fetal
position beneath his desk, thinking of fountains and baby
diapers.

> *Every time I see road-kill in the neighborhood or on the
> freeway, I imagine the visual paired with its soundtrack, and
> the music that is playing in my head is always "Saturday
> Night" by the Bay City Rollers. The skunks, the squirrels,
> the crimson and fur, the spots on the pavement several
> inches away from the bulk of the mess, removed from the
> slaughtered carcass to take on a new life and meaning in
> death and divorce. This is the place where humans collide
> with the other side, I think; this is the place where it will
> happen: the meat and the flesh, the two animal worlds
> overlapping, carnage, a kind of ferocious tourism...*

There is always the idea that a transformation must be
made, a development into the unknown, a change that will
facilitate a kind of rebirth. From reverie to fulfillment, that
is the shift in the whole thing, the marching into alterity
and therefore, the birth of his will. And so, in the comfort
of diapers, he made the afternoons of several weekends
pass amicably through one neighborhood garage sale after

another, in search of childhood bicycles and perhaps a few answers, as well. After the span of a month, maybe more, he discovered the vehicle, or at the very least, a reasonable facsimile, and purchased the bike for around seventeen dollars.

He took the tiny bicycle home, walked alongside it on the sidewalk, closer and closer to his home, all the while not wondering about the constant shift in the location of his furniture, all the while thinking about the smoothness in the texture of raw meat. He was almost afraid, now that the journey had begun, to go any farther, the *fear* of what might be inside the gift box greater than the *desire* to see what it might be. Walking it into the comfort of his living room, he positioned the bike between himself and the television, splitting the focus of his eyes constantly from one to the other, and back again.

Days went by, in much the same manner, and slowly, it dawned on him that it was a journey that must be made, a physicality that must be realized. He walked down the block to the supermarket, diaper in hand, and asked the butcher for enough ground meat to loosely form the shape of the white vessel in his hands. The butcher acquiesced. In the living room chair, the smiles that had washed over him from the market back to his home slowly faded. How could he have expected the meat to stay in one place? The shy and clumsy frame of the ground meat crumbled, anxiously breaking free at its first chance to submit to the whims of gravity.

Information found scribbled on a post-it note on the fridge:

Must purchase from the Store:

Heavy-duty surgical needles, one dozen

New package, large adult white diapers

120 lb. test line, suitable for large game fishing

Enough flank steak, raw, needed to customize an adult-sized diaper

The lights from the television animated the lines in the bicycle, but he was far too busy to pay attention at this point. Slumped in his lap, couched in the white foam of the adult diaper, laid the twenty-five or so pounds of raw flank steak. The grimace on the face of the butcher would have been enough to kill the cow. No matter, for the construction of the beef diaper was well underway, and thank goodness, for the meat included its own roadmap for rot and decay. Sewing eagerly, he pricked his fingers several times, and felt the sting of glory each time he did; the diaper began to take shape, first with hesitation, the rear, the sides, the holes for the legs forming eagerly now, evolution taking over. Nothing could deter him; he was his own question mark, the punctuation in the sentence of the moment, poised on its own edge of whiteness. Breathing deeply, he lifted the slouching pink diaper upwards, its sagging girth mimicking the curve in the smile on his lips. Whatever it was, it made him happy.

Three or four splinters of light shone through the openings in the drapes; soon it would be morning, the stumbling neighbors clumsily rolling out to their cars and onto the freeway. If he was going to make this trip, the time was now.

He swung one leg over the seat of the bike, a lazy motion resembling the movements of a man on a wet carpet wearing only socks. The bike was much lower than he thought it would be, and thankfully so, as the damp tonnage of the diaper anchored him in the seat, beckoning his rear towards a lower and lower resting place. The beef diaper slipped warmly into the shape of the old bicycle seat, the lines of the glen plaid suit shifting slowly as he raised first one foot to a plastic pedal, then the other. Jerking through the door of the house, he moved confidently towards the freeway down the other end of the block, the sun slowly rising on this day.

To begin a journey is to walk midstream into a loop of every journey that has ever been taken by every other brave human being. And so it was this time. Riding hesitantly onto the freeway, the rising curve of the pavement cresting upwards from underneath him, he discovered exhilaration, the likes of which he was sure he had never felt before. In the slack of the damp beef, he felt the comfort of belonging, the rightness of being, and parading onto the slowest lane of the freeway, he was almost immediately guided back off onto the next offramp, the two lanes colliding to become the same. Riding off of the freeway, laughing as the breeze, quietly whispering, danced past his ears, he heard the song of his belonging, and followed the street around the block and back onto the freeway onramp, only to do this again, and again, and again....

STORIES LEADING UP TO, AND SOME INCLUDING, E. LEON SPAUGHY

Several months ago, I began to notice that I was being followed by a skunk. First, across the street from my car somewhere in the foothills beneath the Hollywood sign, while on my way to get a late night cup of coffee. As I took a few steps away from my car door, I heard something scumbling around in the bushes, and although it was dark, I sincerely did not believe that it sounded like the scumbling of a cat or dog. Dropping a box of cookies or crackers, well that sounds like canine scumbling. Stepping into a small patch of dry pine needles, maybe one could mistake this for feline scumbling. But this was more like the sound of a fat child inhaling a Twinkie, something far more mysterious and bodily.

After crossing the street maybe a block and a half from the coffee shop, I realized that back over on the other side, ambling along in a parallel direction, was the small black-and-white creature commonly called a skunk. Furthermore, whenever I stopped to look over at it, the animal paused in its tracks too, and lazily looked over at me, an uncanny mirror of my curiosity. He had a dark, oily tuft of hair arching up into a small unsightly clump, ending down around his eyes. Our first mutual sighting, no words exchanged.

Later in that same month, I parked my car in front of my house perhaps twenty-five or so miles from the scene of the original sighting; this was about three in the morning after a late weekend night at a party with friends. As I took the first of a few steps towards the front door and up the little hill in the front lawn, the familiar body of the good-sized black-and-white animal sauntered out in front of me, cautiously looked up from a distance of not more than eight feet, and then (prematurely?) turned to walk back into the bushes without fear or hesitation. A second sighting, without a single line of conversation.

After that point, I began to notice a strange trend occur. It seemed that after the first two sightings, the image of the skunk clearly manifested itself in my waking life, nearly every day. Pictures on t-shirts, logos on the sides of enormous shipping trucks, posted on a flyer somewhere in the Russian district of the city, and of course, the occasional actual sighting of the beast. I was convinced that not only was this the same animal creeping around in the margins of my life, but also that if I remained patient, eventually the skunk would voice its intentions, making its presence entirely clear. That same night, I could smell the pungent odor of him as I cruised around the freeway off-ramp in the direction of my home.

Eventually, after months of such encounters, the small animal approached me in the backyard one evening while I was jotting a few notes down at the glass-topped table beneath the apple tree. After professionally writing marketing copy for more than a decade, I was busy working on a short descriptive paragraph for a furniture magazine catalog, desperately trying to think of another word for beige. I'd been in a fever of loneliness and vexation ever since my wife left me, hardly noticing that an entire year had elapsed since her departure.

Being alone had been anguishing, varying among degrees of being unbearable, and the vast majority of my friends had also temporarily disappeared, probably sensing my overt neediness, and cowering in repulsion. I understood this reaction. After all, when one wants so much more than any one person can ever offer in the way of salvation, most people opt to give up rather than to try and then fail. I might have done exactly the same.

"And as for myself, I have never met a Mormon who did not have a trampoline in their backyard. And if they did not, well then they knew someone who did: *Another* Mormon. And so on goes my point," retorted the little creature E. Leon Spaughy, approaching me in the backyard as if in the middle of a long speech on the recreational habits of certain religious peoples.

I couldn't think of what to add to the conversation at that point. I wasn't so much surprised by the fact that he was speaking to me, but that it had taken as long as it did for him to manifest in my presence. I pondered this as I let his last line hang there, in mid-air, much the way a person must feel at the high point on a swing: momentarily without connection to anything, and then jerked back into the present almost maliciously, to deal with reality. I focused on E. Leon's bewhiskered little face. The reality of the situation? I was speaking with a skunk. "Why are you here?"

"Well, when the student is ready, you know what they say," he replied with a knowing smile and hollow, melancholy eyes.

"Uhhh—no, I actually don't. Have you been following me?" I asked, only slightly unnerved.

"Your teacher has arrived, don't you see? And no—following seems much too drastic a version of what's been happening. Let's just say, we've almost caught up to each other many times of late, but only now were you ready to begin this conversation." His confidence seemed to stem from a wisdom that emanated from deep within him. He was decrepit, beyond years though—not worn down in the traditional sense, more like bearing the weight of many long years of wandering and seeing the world.

"Are we to be friends then? I mean—will you have a seat here with me?" I had almost forgotten my manners after being taken by surprise. As I asked him to join me, E. Leon was already scampering up into the chair across from me. He proceeded to lean over the table, perched on his hind limbs, and pulled my small black notebook over, losing himself wholeheartedly in the pages and pages of my notes.

He had an odd way of speaking, his upper lip held firm against a trembling lower jaw and I could tell his teeth were rotting, and not all there. "I have been admiring your gardening habits for some time now, and must admit—I find myself quite taken with the strength of your vocabulary," he slushed out, burping almost unnoticeably out of the side of his mouth as he closed the notebook and slid it in my direction.

His accent was British, refined—more elegant than I had imagined it would be. You see, given the depths of my loneliness, this was not at all unexpected, and certainly not a situation I was prepared to reject. I had indeed wondered about what we might discuss together, the little old beast and myself, and taking tea in the evenings had certainly been on my mind. Much the same way a child raises up an imaginary friend, houses him in his closet and brings him out into the world to share the child's often overwhelming experience of things, I had thought a great deal about the little skunk, E. Leon Spaughy, as a friend. I blushed when he said this; it was flattering. "I believe tawny is the word you're looking for," he said humbly.

E. Leon was proving himself quite useful already. Without much effort, we became fast friends, spending a great deal of time together almost immediately after his introduction and proposal. Given his avuncular nature and instant familiarity, it was something like being visited by an old, wealthy and cultured relative, formerly long-lost and then magically—suddenly there.

§ § §

Last weekend was by far the most interesting two days of my life. Ever since this new friendship began, though I had no idea it would only take a few short days to get comfortable with the idea of it, I had spent my time in total relaxation, investigating curious things around the edges of the city. These were the parts of town that E. Leon unflinchingly referred to as "the Badlands." He had casually moved into my place after that first day, and usually awoke around two in the afternoon. Then, he would make me lift him into the passenger seat of my car to go for an adventure, mounting his snout somewhere on the front of the dashboard with the air conditioning ruffling up his tuft of hair. His tiny joints creaked a bit, but he never winced.

Thursday around two-fifteen, an interesting story was broadcast over the radio on NPR. The details of the story were minimal, but the location where the story had taken place sounded familiar. It seemed that a couple of reporters had found an old car graveyard and junk shop, outdoors, in an area surrounding the southeastern border of town where the wrecking fields and shipping graveyards lay nearly dormant, producing rusted-out rubble resembling oversized mountains of metallic candy.

Saturday morning I took tea with E. Leon, who buried his snout in the cup, burping occasionally, as I watched curls of steam climb elegantly up his nose. Shortly after, he decided it might be fun to take a trip to the same junkyard in the story, muttering something like, "Perhaps we shall embark on a little adventure of our own." He grinned, utterly defining mischievousness. It was looks like that one that confirmed my belief that he was well on in years, as if his dainty manner of climbing in and out of the car or the bed was not enough to draw the conclusion.

When we arrived, it was nearly exactly the way I had imagined from the radio story: masses of old cars, rusted and bruised, heaped in colored piles on each other like brooding, Rockwell-esque siblings frozen in front of the television, angling for a better view of the screen or for swift possession over the remote control. I opened the door for E. Leon to exit the car, offering more assistance than usual as I managed to pick him up behind his forelegs, which were resting on the dash, and set him on the ground. He was only slightly larger than a cat of average girth.

We scattered. E. Leon moved off to the west end of the yard, and I moved north, straight into the thick of it. After what must have been several hours, I began to hear his calling voice, familiar as that of a relative, even in its muffled state. After locating the direction that his call was coming from, I hurried through the maze of junked automobiles, all somehow appearing to be twice the size of functional cars I saw daily on the roads, only to discover E. Leon.

He was face-down, his curious little snout temporarily entombed halfway down into the backseat of an old root beer brown Chevelle, some hundred and a half yards from where we first entered. His paws were making it a bit difficult for him to get at just what he thought he had seen, which turned out to be an old, water-stained envelope,

160

about ten inches by five, sealed with a half-broken tooth hinge that practically fell off in my hand when I tugged at it. Inside was the most curious thing.

Photos of an old man and a few pieces of living room furniture strewn about the hallway of what appeared to be an aged, partially dilapidated house, told a fractured story in a sequence of Polaroids that E. Leon and I shuffled hurriedly back and forth for a short while. In one series, the old man, face wrinkled like an old wallet, did what looked like a series of superhero acrobatic tricks: half-draped over an arm chair in one, practically upside-down in mid-air over the couch in another, two spoons clasped angrily, one in each hand, poised in front of the camera for a close-up shot like some kind of demon in a third. He wore nothing but tube socks and a tee shirt in most of the photos, with a kind of loincloth that looked like it was knitted or crocheted, two little balls on strings dangling like two red cherries over the waist.

Another shot showed him with a silvery pile of nickels in a mound between his out-stretched arms at the breakfast table, a pushed-away plate showing the remains of two half-eaten fried eggs and a burnt piece of toast. His smile was broken, jagged teeth poking through a shaggy little thing you might call a beard. It was magic.

We tucked the photos back into their envelope, poked around a little more at the junkyard, and headed off in the direction of home. We stopped for a tea when we got closer; that was around five in the evening. "I have to catch the McLaughlin Hour tonight," E. Leon snipped over his shoulder as he headed towards the guest bedroom where he had slept since he began staying with me. When he slept in the bed each night, he stained the sheets so miserably with his natural pungent odors that I had to throw them out several times in the last month already. But what could I do; he was like family returned from the grave somehow.

§ § §

One day some months later, I was standing stiff at the waist in the kitchen of my home, which overlooked the cul-de-sac of my block out front. It had been several hours since I'd awoken, but E. Leon, I believed, was still asleep, as was his customary habit. Washing grapes in a white plastic strainer seated beneath the cold running water, I watched the glass-green bulbs of stemmed fruit bead up, repelling the water's attempt to drown them. It was somewhat mesmerizing, until my stare was broken suddenly, and my eyes shot up, engaged by haphazard motion somewhere in my periphery. The motion seemed to be coming from somewhere low to the ground, and then I noticed beyond the window in front of me, an elderly man lying slack and prone in the middle of the street outside my house.

He was writhing around like an overturned beetle and making no obvious progress towards the integrity of typical upright, human motion. Moments passed and I did nothing, motionless and watching him instead, taken in by the cinematic view through my kitchen window and paralyzed somehow by the pathetic nature of the situation taking place out in the street. Time seemed irrelevant— none of this even seemed real to me.

Just then, I noticed E. Leon moving in quick steps, a Muybridge photographic essay put back into real-time motion, heading out of the front door and down the stairs towards the street. Suddenly, he was standing over the old man, while I was still in the kitchen, immobilized and then ashamed, until I trailed out into the street to offer some assistance to my old friend who couldn't possibly raise this man back up on his own. The first thing I noticed was the smell as I approached the two of them. It must have been ninety degrees, and the hot air was dry, palpable, hanging with a creepy lightness like stacks of oven-baked saltine crackers looming in the sky around us.

I smelled perspiration, which was slightly sweet, almost metallic, bitter fruit preserves gone stale. I swung around next to E. Leon and behind the doddering old man, shriveled in the places his clothes didn't cover, like piles of blanched yellow raisins. He was more than scared, but E. Leon reassured him with all the confidence of a paramedic or seasoned military man in the middle of battle. I'm not sure how long he had been laying in the street, or who would have helped him had E. Leon not selflessly come to his rescue, or whether or not he ever would have been able to make it back up on his own. I think the man lived next door, or else somewhere on the block. None of us spoke. There was no point in asking him if he was okay, but I thought about it, and knew that he couldn't be. A quick glance over to E. Leon confirmed this thought, with his compassionate stare trained on the old man lying there in front of him.

I smelled the minty plastic odor of an evergreen after-shave coming off the old man in waves, given the profusion of sweat and fear being released in abundant perspiration droplets from off the surface of his skin, which appeared mottled and leathery. E. Leon's paws clutched beneath the old man's left arm, as he tried to bolster him up slightly from his side, all the while providing some measure of comfort to me that I was not in this alone. Given the weight of the old man and the comparatively small size of the skunk, his efforts were proving wasteful at best.

As if rehearsing some kind of high school wrestling position, or else an old-time vaudeville routine, I hinged both my arms into ninety-degree angles, hands up, closed-fisted, and hooked them underneath the old man's armpits as E. Leon stepped out of the way to our left. The old man was thoroughly damp, the totality of which I noticed then for the first time. "Don't you be scared," I said, craning my entire body over him, preparing to lunge upward. I don't think he heard me at that point, or maybe he was really too scared to pay attention to whatever was not happening immediately inside of him. E. Leon must have gone around behind the two of us, as I had temporarily lost sight of him. Completely engaged in my rescue at this point, I was not certain I would have been able to keep track of him anyway.

It was like a life-sized puppeteering act then, all limp arms and legs on the old man's part, dangling heavily as if on the knot somehow, tied into complex series of levers and pulleys that I was almost controlling from behind him. He was too heavy for this, mostly dead weight. "You need to help—I can't do this by myself," I muttered to the back of his head, which was covered with salt and pepper hair, thinned and thoroughly damp with sweat.

I noticed a tiny maroon rivulet of blood working its way down from underneath the blue mesh baseball cap he was wearing. Being an average-sized man, this sort of activity was taxing and overwhelming, demanding of practically all my physical strength. "Take a deep breath now. Breathe." He needed to listen to me: I had control over the situation, and wouldn't let go until he'd been returned to safety. The decision had come from somewhere unconscious inside of me, but this was definitely what was happening at that point.

There was just then a breeze taking over, only slightly, and on it rested the smells of both dried cypress and fresh urine, like an old cat's litter box. Out of fear, the old man had probably accidentally pissed himself, or maybe I just noticed this and it had happened much earlier. I couldn't see around the front of him to tell for sure, and his legs were buckling every time we got even remotely close to standing upright. There—now he was standing up straight—well, a kind of straightness where the center of gravity was closer to his wobbly ankles than his midsection, where it was supposed to be. I was feeling something beyond sympathy for the old man; I could see myself in him somehow. We had both fallen, were both pathetic and in need of help from some force greater than ourselves. With this fact in mind, I decided that I liked him: *We were the same thing.* Maybe I didn't even mean that, or couldn't completely realize the weight of the thought, but I was thinking exactly that, in short, terse sentences, repeating it over and over in the back of my mind.

The old man's feet were self-propelled, scuttling aimlessly in an overwrought attempt to move in a straight line pointed at his front door. Any fragment of gravel in the street caused him to lose his balance; his breathing was frantic. "Don't push me," he whispered in a coarse manner. I eased up when he said this—it was the first thing he had told me, and his voice somehow came out and disappeared quickly, a feather blown off his tongue. There was no gravity in it. I wondered for a second if he had said anything at all, and I leaned back a little, allowing him to lean back onto me in the process. My arms were covered in sweat: I didn't know whose it was.

"Slow down, old man," I urged.

"Don't," he said.

"We can take all day if you need it," I reassured.

"Don't," he repeated.

It took almost an hour to complete the walk, which was only really twenty feet from the street to the old man's porch, which ended up definitely being next door to E. Leon and me. He was barely propped upright, sitting still, many degrees beyond winded. I was standing in front of him, brow furled, arms crossed, staring into his face. There was a blankness there. Maybe he was embarrassed, maybe he just didn't know any better. "You need water; I'll get it for you."

As I returned to my house, I suddenly realized the full weight of E. Leon's absence, and wondered if he was also back in the house. I took a quick tour of the house to see if he was in any of the rooms or backyard, and he was nowhere to be found. I quickly snatched up a couple of water bottles from the refrigerator, still singular in my rescue mission and intent on completing my task. E. Leon, I could find later.

It had been difficult to leave the old man there by himself; while in my house those few moments, I pictured finding him on the ground next to his green plastic lawn chair, necessitating a repeat of the last hour of our lives together. When I returned with the bottles of water, I thought to open one for him so that he would not have to. I wondered if he could even have opened it up on his own, as his hands were trembling, more than slightly. He didn't say thank you—he just drank.

"You cut the back of your head. Make sure someone takes a look at that, old man." He didn't care, or he didn't want to hear it. I couldn't stay with him anymore at that point – and I knew I had done all I could for him, or at least all that he would let me do. "I'm leaving you now. Don't move 'til someone comes home for you. Someone's coming here for you, yes?" He was still drinking, holding the small water bottle to the edge of his lips, which were flaked and scaly, too dry.

He said nothing to me, looking up in my direction but somehow through me, way past where I was standing; I left him there. Hours later in my living room, I realized, as the immediacy of the events of the day began to fade, that E. Leon hadn't been around for quite a long while. And it would stay that way; I would eventually come to find out—E. Leon had taken his leave of me as mysteriously and suddenly as he had first appeared. Alone in my home once again, I walked over to the telephone in the entry hall, and picked up the receiver. Slowly, I dialed the first number that came to my mind. There were friends in the world whom I suddenly missed.

CONRAD "CONNIE" BORSCHT ON LOOKING

Why He Looks the Way He Looks: Darby Ammon

You can be sitting in a darkened theater during the previews of certain movies, and just for a second, you can forget everything you might have known about the movie you were going to see. If you're lucky enough, you can dupe yourself into believing that the movie is about to unfold right before your very eyes, as if it were being broadcast from a live feed somewhere on the other side of the globe, in real time. As if not a single frame of the film was ever cut, sliced and taped back together somewhere in a dark corner of a film lab in Hollywood. That straightjacket moment of utter placeless-ness turns the cool dark of the theater inside out, almost white, a hint of blindness from shining a flashlight for too long into your eyes. When everyone in the movie house suddenly disappears, the interminable clicking of the projector's shutter becoming less like a noise and more like... maybe a color. Darby thinks this exact moment is "Gray."

Moments like this are not at all uncommon for Darby Ammon, who was practically born a cynic. Sitting on the living room floor, he cocks his head a bit to the right, forcing the air-cooled gusts from the a.c. to blow back the front of his hair in the shape of a half-shell. He's been sitting there for twenty-two minutes now; morning is officially over, the noontime sun hanging overhead on a stiff broil for everything underneath. The carpets have dug out bumpy circular impressions in both of his knees, which he fingers around, feeling alien flesh. He looks down at his fingers; his left foot is asleep. He's tried before to get his limbs to fall asleep all in unison, to mimic what it might be like to be a paraplegic, to get the thing to happen regularly, like a paycheck or breakfast. Sprawled starfish-like over the kitchen chair, he lets the metal arms dig notches into the spaces under his arms, behind his knees, choking up the flow of blood and oxygen or whatever else. So far, the best he's done was a leg-arm combo, and this only after a dozen attempts—nothing close to what he'd set as his goal.

Darby was only ten years old the first time he was scammed. A family friend, Doctor Corky Rosenstamp, a doctor of the eyes, made false claims in the way of his vision, and more to the point, claimed that Darby was nearly blind. In order to fix this, he received a two-pound pair of brown plastic glasses, semi-rounded in the lens and half an inch thick. Once a week, Darby would get dropped off at the eye doctor's office, where he would be forced through a highly structured battery of ocular examinations. A large metallic apparatus would swing down from somewhere in the ceiling overhead, robotic in nature with a single elbow-shaped hinge in the middle, configured like an enormous black metallic arm. The room would go dark, and he could pretend like he was alone, in that darkened space of the movie theater.

Darby remembers the cold black metal on his face, more chilled-muted than freezing. A series of red and green lenses would be slipped into the machine, providing him with a kind of three-D multi-layered picture, maybe two dogs standing next to a pair of low shrubs, which he would then have to try to force-focus back into one single image. After three years of this, the story broke one day in the news that Dr. Rosenstamp was actually a phony. Darby had been duped, and his mother made the decision to get him tested again at a different facility some time after the media stopped dragging Rosenstamp's name through the press. Not all was lost, though. It seemed that all the years of corrective examinations had provided Darby with better than perfect vision: Dr. Rosenstamp had turned Darby into a professional looker.

On his way towards the bathroom, he knocks over a pint glass of water, full from the night before, resting on the floor near the a.c. He pauses for a second to acknowledge the mishap, squashed into the slow-mo version of blaring summer heat, then stumbles two feet farther and empties his bladder into the bowl below. Returning to the living room, Darby tries standing in the wet puddle to see if it will make him have to pee again, only seconds after the first time. He looks upward at the ceiling, mouth hanging open like a drawbridge, eyes glazing towards a corner somewhere behind him. It's a pose he thinks he may have seen in a slick French film once, a pose that he is remembering helped a man to pee. When he dropped out of high school a few years ago, Darby spent a lot of time hanging out around the house while his mother was away working as a legal clerk at a small-time law firm that was dedicated mostly to getting DUI cases thrown out of court. Swing shift meant alone time for young Darby, principal creator of his own small universe. As soon as she would leave for work mid- to late-morning, he would linger around inside for a while, then trail out of the house in the direction of town, past the used car junkyards and the gigantic citrus processing plants, tasting the orangey odor somewhere deep inside his nose almost always. It was on one of those walks that Darby met his first boss, Connie Borscht. He didn't have to look too hard, either.

A Day on the Set With Connie Borscht: Point of View, Darby Ammon

A middle-aged man named Conrad "Connie" Borscht runs an underground kiddy porn slash snuff film ring in a neighborhood somewhere north of Los Angeles, near Valencia. Named after orange groves that patched up the sides of all the roads like two-toned quilts, the city of Valencia fell prey to the city's more undesirable characters, who fled there in dramatic numbers during the great citrus boom of the late seventies and early eighties. Every out-of-work hoodlum from Van Nuys to Sylmar hopped into his chalk white van conversion and headed out of the Valley due north, and all this over a period of roughly five years. Picking oranges was a Godsend for parties interested in criminal behavior. It provided the perfect cover by day. They came from towns where everything was kept up on cinder blocks out in the front yard. Most of the time, only the car was up on blocks. If things were really bad, sometimes the house would be up on blocks. And when the whole world was about to sink into the crapper, well then chickens, ponies, garden hoses, even the dogs with no legs would be out in the front yard, all up on blocks.

The Valley's deserters had set their collective mind on profiting from what had come to be regarded as the single greatest agricultural explosion since the discovery of elephant garlic up in Gilroy decades earlier. A cultural phenomenologist had referred to the discovery of mutant super-sized oranges bigger than basketballs as "Otters," which stood for "Oranges ThaT double as Everything ReceptacleS," which they repeated in news reports as often as possible back then. Back then, there was so much orange juice in the world, developers had started to think of alternative uses for the knobby, hollowed-out fruits, like strange purses and dried citrus luggage. Ten years after the short orange boom, small police flyers were going up in the town at least once a week. Whatever orange trees hadn't been bulldozed (to allow for the freeways and condominium developments) got covered with them. "Pedophile in town, be on the lookout, kiddy porn king answers to the name 'Connie,'" the latest ones said.

Conrad "Connie" had fuzzy hair like brown-mottled q-tips on the top and the sides, wrinkled ears that sort of pigeon-toed themselves inward at the tops and bottoms, and four-day-old beard growth on his face that connected around the corners to the fuzz on the back of his neck. Connie was actually not a kiddy porn maker, nor was he a purveyor of snuff films. But then no one has ever made a movie that was actually real, anyway. Connie's films just looked real to most people—he knew how to use the medium to trick the eye, to take people's senses into his own trust, and then completely take advantage of them. Connie's main male lead was a five-foot-four-inch tall freckled twenty-four year old who looked more like he was twelve. On camera, that is. Plastic was the end goal for Connie when choosing his actors; they all had to look vaguely like prosthetic human dolls. Shiny, slippery skin that looked more like silicone stretched taut over stiff skeletons. On camera, they read as pre-teens. It wasn't until they actually opened their mouths to speak that you realized their bodily orifices were not "just barely hollow," or molded shut completely.

Pygma Meadows came out to Los Angeles from West Virginia to become a famous actor. All his fans say he looks amazing when he's covered in blood. He's sifted through a hundred letters that all say the same thing. Pygma's real-life failure, the fact that he looks like a little kid who is made out of translucent plastic, makes him Connie's greatest asset. When he arrives on the set in the morning, he is quiet, stoic. The small crew knows how he gets on the days during shooting when he has to stab someone or beat them over the head with a baseball bat. Someone hands him coffee. He is smoking a cigarette at the table in the fake kitchen when Connie comes in, flops down into the chair next to him, and starts walking Pygma through the scene he has to shoot today.

Pygma's female co-star on the set is named Clara
Latch. Her tiny nose and streak-white skin are topped off
with a staticky mop of thin-ish blonde hair that all adds up
to her looking like a duckling. Pygma says Clara's mouth
is like a miniature blown-up balloon; he says her lip-gloss
tastes like Fruit Loops, and the indentation below her nose
feels like a tiny patch of suede. Clara told Connie yesterday
that Pygma's breath was as rancid as the two-year-old sack
of rotting potatoes she found beneath the kitchen sink last
month in her girlfriend's house. Thousands of tiny black
spots turned into gnats that flew up at them the second
the two girls reached into the cabinet to pick up the sack of
dead potatoes. Connie told her that meant she was probably
a better actor than he had originally imagined. Clara
smiled, creasing up faintly in the outer corners of her eyes.

There is quiet on the set. No one can be heard
breathing here, not even Clara. Pygma sits next to her
on the edge of the bed; he has just finished a scene at the
kitchen table, where he had to eat his cereal from the bowl,
tracing in mid-air, tightly squared right angles with his
spoon. Pygma's hands are on either side of Clara's neck
now, his body has half-curved in towards her on the bed,
with one foot now craned over his other knee. Everything
on the set is beige. Pygma wears a coffee-stained brown
t-shirt, camel colored corduroy slacks, tan socks and light
brown shoes. Clara's skimpy tank is a fawny golden brown,
and her skirt and sandals are matching milky-taupe. The
bed linens, the blanket, the carpets in front of the bed—all
a soft, buttery ochre. The nightstand table is a blond pine;

the butterfly clip in the side of Clara's hair is golden. There is a postcard of two men wrestling on the wall directly over the bed, their bodies contorted into the shape of an oversized, irregular arm, hinge-curved at the middle, with one body slumped on top of the other. There is a drop of blood in the corner of the carpet.

They begin kissing. More like nuzzling at first, puppy-dogging each other's necks and shoulders with their noses. This goes on for some time until the first kiss, Clara initiating contact with a vaguely splashy noise from her mouth. The room becomes all wet mouth noise now, the kissing mounting in pressure. Pygma stops in mid-contact, awkwardly hustles off his shoes, and piles Clara's legs onto his own. Seconds later, they are kissing again, and he arches her legs over him, shoving her fully on the bed behind him. She is not nervous. None of this is real.

Pygma is equal parts plastic doll, thesis on freckles, and all elbows. He is on her now; she is molding the sides of his head like she's crumpling a newspaper. Somewhere in the middle of all this, he has tucked his right hand in under the pillow next to her head and pulled out an ice pick, nearly eight inches long, which hangs in mid-air now in front of the camera. His clutching hand barely reveals the few red swirls written into the handle of the instrument, reading parts of "Coca-Cola." Clara is still; her hand rises up, as if to say no. Her lips are parted gently. There is saliva on her cheek. Suddenly... Blood everywhere.

Why Darby Thinks Looking Sounds the Way It Does: Connie's Recipe for Exploding Heads

Here's how you make an exploding head:

First thing you do is you take the person who you want to make the replica head of, and take a full head mold of that person. You do this by applying a bald cap to the person carefully, and then applying some Vaseline to their eyebrows. Preferably this person has no facial hair. You then take something called dental alginate, of a type known as Prosthetic Grade Cream, or P.G.C. This is a powder that is mixed with water. You have a five-minute set time. While that paste that you have made with the alginate is still wet, you put it over the entirety of the face. You try to make an even coating about a quarter of an inch thick over the entire head; that will set up very quickly. You should allow space around the nostrils for the person to breathe. This is then covered in a two-part shell of plastic gauze, which is the same sort of plaster-impregnated gauze used for making casts for your arm, you know, for a broken bone. It is a two-part cast, a front and a back, so that you can pop it off. Once the plaster sets, you pop it off, you slit the back of the alginate with a knife, and pull the person out of the alginate. You then put it back into the plaster encasement, so that it holds its shape. This is then filled with molten clay. The molten clay is made by melting in a hot pot: one part beeswax to four parts non-sulfur clay, such as Chavante or Roma Plastilina. Once the clay sets, it may be removed from the alginate, and the alginate can be discarded. The clay head is then chased and finished to take out any imperfections. You then make a silicone mold of this head with a fiberglass jacket, or "mother mold." Once you have this mold, you get something called Geleffex. You then heat the Geleffex in a double boiler until it's a liquid form; it's a dense gelatin. You pour it into the mold, and slush-cast it, which means you roll it around just coating the surface, not filling the mold entirely. Once you have a good solid layer of gelatin in there, you allow it to cool and solidify. You then slush cast it with Ultracal. The Ultracal will dry very hard. At this point you will have a gelatin layer, with the plaster layer inside; it will then be hollow. The gelatin may be tinted to a flesh tone prior to casting. You then go to the butcher shop and buy a cow's brain, or a calf's brain. You fill that hollow head, while it is still in the mold, with the calf's brain and some fake blood, and a bunch of nurnies. Nurnies are random bits of flesh-like stuff made from a thin layer of latex painted onto glass and then peeled off and shredded. Nurnies are sometimes also referred to as nubbins. This is then capped off with a layer of poly-foam, or plaster, or Ultracal, to seal the brains and blood inside. You then remove it from the mold, and paint the head with grease paint to finish its appearance like flesh. The benefit of the Geleffex is that it looks already translucent like flesh does, and has the sort of springiness of flesh, and holds the detail of the skin that will be in the mold. You then buy a wig to fit to the head. The wig should be scored in the back, so that when the head is hit with a baseball bat, the wig tears and allows the insides to come out. Once the wig is fitted on, you hit the thing with a baseball bat, and the head explodes. The Geleffex tears,

178

the plaster functions like a skull, shatters, bits of fake bone (which are actually the Ultracal) go flying, and of course, the nurnies, blood and calf's brain go flying, as well.

One of Connie's Movies Gets Reviewed

TRANSLUCENT AND NEEDY

By E.O. Hippis, Critic for the Milwaukee Daily Bugle

Running Time, 42 minutes, 2001

Although it would be quite easy, and even perhaps somewhat correct, to argue that Conrad "Connie" Borscht's new film "Translucent and Needy" is saturated with a kind of human longing, something vaguely sweet and tolerably romantic, I am of the opinion that it is generally more valid to say that the film exudes a creepy kind of stillness. The kind of peace or calm that is generally associated with a sense of eeriness and alarm. During the duration of the film, I couldn't shake the kind of nervous tension that speaks to the idea that one is seeing something one is not supposed to see. The camera decidedly will not look away; we are being privileged with a kind of looking that we are not supposed to have.

Perhaps in watching underage, translucent bodies that romp, eat, copulate, sleep and die, something seemingly sly and misguided bubbles to the surface. Surely there is a sense of romantic allure in the slackness of the human body shut down, but in Borscht's film, there exists more a sense of noir, inasmuch as it is the kind of thing one might shudder to look at while simultaneously not being able to turn away. (In some part, this explains the huge European successes that have come to Borscht in his eleven-year career, though he continues to be marginalized in America. The films seem to appeal to the "banal as bittersweet" attitude that exists as a given in overseas culture). In "Translucent and Needy," one watches the figure intensely, as in watching a dead body from just behind police lines at a murder scene, not calmly, all the while imagining that someone else will come over and catch us looking, immediately asking or forcing us to look away. In eleven years of filmmaking, no one has ever been able to prove whether Borscht's films are real or fake.

Because of this feeling of creepy stillness, I think about the intended audience for the piece, and I am led to believe that perhaps the only person who belongs in front of this film is the person who stars in the film: Pygma Meadows, watching himself on film. The idea does not surprise me. I was the first critic to refer to Borscht as "an ailing humanist with a penchant for mirrors" (from *Smaller Features on Film,* an Underground Zine, December 1990). Human beings are plagued with immediate and sometimes maddening limitations, many of them focusing on the visual aspect of the senses. All the things that we cannot see are things that might tell us a great deal about ourselves. We will never see ourselves in the mirror with our eyes closed just as we will never see ourselves the way we will look when we are dead—the same way that Pygma Meadows will never really see himself when he is sleeping, murdering or copulating. What would this tell us about the condition of being human that is specifically ours? All the events of our lives that happen when our eyes are closed… they remain in the vision and memories of other bodies remote and separate from our own.

Complicating matters further, Connie Borscht seems to emphasize in many of the shots, the abstract nature of the body: locations are made to look ambiguous, one cannot tell the hips from the ribs as they sandwich in the stomach, and something is nearly always completely reduced to a shadow. The body becoming landscape. Pygma's freckled body lies slack in one memorable shot of the film, and just for a moment, looks like the awkward and limp form of a blood-speckled white plastic garbage bag. The body becomes other in the inanimate states that Borscht forces them into. In this way, too, a person is categorically and comprehensively *reduced* in these states: sleep, eyes closed in the mirror, death. With the eyes closed, the body, as in sleep, becomes a shadow of itself, a kind of surrogate or reversal. Meaning is drained from the self, parts that are unknowable to us are revealed… But in this moment where the opportunity to see and know ourselves exists, the body is deflated and unaware, a step behind and out of reach, a victim of its own limitations. Of course, during all of this, the camera unflinching, watches everything. Some say that Connie's films should be considered unwatchable and criminal; I say the only horrific thing about this film is that the camera, desperately inhuman, refuses to ever look away.

ABOUT THE AUTHOR

Matty Byloos was born in Los Angeles in 1974 and attended Santa Clara University and the Art Center College of Design. His first collection of short stories, *Don't Smell the Floss,* comprises work written in the years after graduate school. Byloos founded and published the literary zine *Smalldoggies* from 2001-05. His fiction has been published in *Fishwrap, Schtick,* and *Undershorts*; in 2004 he was included in the UCLA Hammer Museum's New American Writing Series; and during 2002-03, he ran the Monday night fiction writing workshop at the Venice Literary Arts Center, Beyond Baroque. In addition, Byloos is an accomplished painter with a history of exhibiting both nationally and internationally. Find out more about Byloos at his website: www.mattybyloos.com. He currently lives and works in Los Angeles.

Photo Credit/Copyright: 2009 Anela Bence-Selkowitz

OTHER GREAT WRITE BLOODY BOOKS

THE GOOD THINGS ABOUT AMERICA
An illustrated, un-cynical look at our American Landscape. Various authors.
Edited by Kevin Staniec and Derrick Brown

JUNKYARD GHOST REVIVAL
with Andrea Gibson, Buddy Wakefield, Anis Mojgani, Derrick Brown, Robbie Q,
Sonya Renee and Cristin O'keefe Aptowicz

THE LAST AMERICAN VALENTINE:
ILLUSTRATED POEMS TO SEDUCE AND DESTROY
24 authors, 12 illustrators team up for a collection of non-sappy love poetry
Edited by Derrick Brown

SOLOMON SPARROWS ELECTRIC WHALE REVIVAL
Poetry Compilation by Buddy Wakefield, Anis Mojgani, Derrick Brown, Dan
Leamen & Mike McGee

STEVE ABEE, GREAT BALLS OF FLOWERS (2009)
New Poems by Steve Abee

SCANDALABRA
New poetry compilation by Derrick Brown

I LOVE YOU IS BACK
Poetry compilation (2004-2006) by Derrick Brown

BORN IN THE YEAR OF THE BUTTERFLY KNIFE
Poetry anthology, 1994-2004 by Derrick Brown

DON'T SMELL THE FLOSS
New Short Fiction Pieces by Matty Byloos

THE CONSTANT VELOCITY OF TRAINS
New Poetry by Lea Deschenes

HEAVY LEAD BIRDSONG
New Poems by Ryler Dustin

UNCONTROLLED EXPERIMENTS IN FREEDOM
New Poems by Brian Ellis

LETTING MYSELF GO
Bizarre God Comedy & Wild Prose by Buzzy Enniss

CITY OF INSOMNIA
New Poetry by Victor D. Infante

WHAT IT IS, WHAT IT IS
Graphic Art Prose Concept book by Maust of Cold War Kids and author Paul Maziar

IN SEARCH OF MIDNIGHT: THE MIKE MCGEE HANDBOOK OF AWESOME
New Poems by Mike McGee

ANIMAL BALLISTICS
New Poetry compilation by Sarah Morgan

NO MORE POEMS ABOUT THE MOON
NON-Moon Poems by Michael Roberts

CAST YOUR EYES LIKE RIVERSTONES INTO THE EXQUISITE DARK
New Poems by Danny Sherrard

LIVE FOR A LIVING
New Poetry compilation by Buddy Wakefield

SOME THEY CAN'T CONTAIN
Classic Poetry compilation by Buddy Wakefield

COCK FIGHTERS, BULL RIDERS, AND OTHER SONS OF BITCHES (2009)
An experimental photographic odyssey by M. Wignall

THE WRONG MAN (2009)
Graphic Novel by Brandon Lyon & Derrick Brown

YOU BELONG EVERYWHERE (2009)
A memoir and how to guide for travelling artists by Derrick Brown with Joel
Chmara, Buddy Wakefield, Marc Smith, Andrea Gibson, Sonya Renee, Anis
Mojgani, Taylor Mali, Mike McGee & more.

WWW.WRITEBLOODY.COM

WRITEBLOODY
QUALITY AMERICAN BOOKS

PULL YOUR BOOKS UP BY THEIR BOOTSTRAPS

Write Bloody Publishing distributes and promotes great books of fiction, poetry and art every year. We are an independent press dedicated to quality literature and book design, with offices in LA and Nashville, TN.

Our employees are authors and artists so we call ourselves a family. Our design team comes from all over America: modern painters, photographers and rock album designers create book covers we're proud to be judged by.

We publish and promote 8-12 tour-savvy authors per year. We are grass-roots, D.I.Y., bootstrap believers. Pull up a good book and join the family. Support independent authors, artists and presses.

Visit us online:
writebloody.com